Catch Me

Catch Me

A Tycoon's Temptation Romance

Michele Arris

TULE
PUBLISHING

Dedication

With love and giant hugs to my A-team

Author's Note

Though inspired by actual places, please note that some events and locations mentioned in this book are fictional and are meant solely for you to escape and enjoy.

Chapter One

"AFTERNOON, ERICA. IS Miss Chase in?" Dominic interrupted the receptionist in the middle of a generous bite of her Jersey Mike's footlong. "I'll just head on back." Her jaws rapidly worked through the mouthful as he started off toward the executive suite.

His patience in short supply, he paid no regard to the heads bobbing up from those stationed within the bullpen of Chase Investments's twenty or so low-wall office cubicles on his march forward.

Beyond the glass-wall partition, he passed the empty executive assistant's desk, crossed glossy maple-wood finishes, and entered Kennedi Chase's office. There, she and his brother, Trenton, sat hemmed together upon the mahogany leather couch, chopsticks working, the smell of spicy beef permeating the moderate-sized corner office. Practically inseparable from the moment they got engaged several months ago, it came as no surprise to find the happy couple together. The timing couldn't be better.

The entire ride over, Dominic had told himself to keep his cool, not to blow his stack, but his frustration must have managed to resurface upon his face. The lovestruck pair's jovial chatter hit a brick wall of silence as they stared back at him, like deer facing fast-approaching high beams.

"Dom, what's wrong?" Trenton stuck the wooden utensils into his takeout and set the carton on the center oak table. He came to the edge of his seat with legs spread and palms braced on his knees. His steel-blue eyes alert, he appeared prepared to take on whatever the battle put before him. "Bro, have a seat."

Related by marriage since the age of five and Trenton age six, Dominic had remained close with his brother even after their parents—his mother and Trenton's father—decided to end their ten-year nuptials.

"Yes, Dom, have some lunch. The bulgogi's really good."

Meeting amber-brown, kind eyes set in features the shade of warm toffee, Dominic took a breath to try to draw on a measure of calm. "Kennedi, you need to talk to your friend, Tabitha. I just left a very pissed off supervisor at the casino construction site. Valerie said Tabitha's been over there again making—"

He paused. Across the room, the bone of his contention stepped out of the adjoining bathroom. An instant heat of anger slid up his spine, wrapped around his neck, and squeezed like a boa. His glare narrowed on the woman who drove his frustration.

"You." He pointed a stiff index finger squarely between her cool, hazel eyes. "I know what you did. You don't have any authority to be giving orders to the construction crew. I've told you not to visit the site without my approval."

"And I've told you, Mr. Balaska, last I checked, you're not my father." The infuriating woman delivered him a slow roll of her eyes—a mannerism he'd ordinarily find fucking sexy had it been any other woman. It was a clear dismissal as she strode to the leather armchair.

She drew that inky, waist-length braid back over her shoulder with a she-devil flair and pinched a snow pea between slender, tawny-tan fingers, munching away before grabbing the carton of soy-glazed brussels sprouts. "I go where I damn well please." She didn't give so much as a glance his way.

Dominic's temper crackled at her blatant disregard. "Not anymore, you don't. I've placed security at the site. If you show up again without prior approval from me, you'll be escorted off the grounds."

Her head snapped up from the smorgasbord of Korean takeout, eyes wide, her pink, pouty lips thinned. "You can't do that!"

"Can and did. Now tell me again what I can't do."

"How about I show you?" A swift flush of color flooding her already naturally blushed cheeks, she jumped to her feet and started to charge at him. Kennedi flung herself up from the couch and blocked her pursuit, holding her back by the shoulders. Shrugging off her friend's grasp, Tabitha side-stepped Kennedi and faced him in full challenge. "Who do you think you are? I have a right to keep track of the construction progress of Chase Confections. It's my store."

Dominic dared her objection with his own. "Progress? Is that what you call changing the blueprints? It's Kennedi's store, too, but you don't see her pressing Valerie with unauthorized and plain old thoughtless changes."

"Thoughtless!" Her aggressive, wide step forward matched his, meeting him essentially toe to toe. Though his six-foot-two frame topped her by about a quarter of a foot given those khaki-colored canvas TOMS on her feet, she held steady, head angled back, her glare precision-sharp with his. "Damn right I changed it," she sneered as that tiny diamond stud glinted like ice fire at the side of her nose. "You're just pissed because I upset your little girlfriend, Valerie."

"Girlfriend?" Eyes closed, grappling for a modicum of patience, he shook his head. "Woman, what are you talking about? Valerie is the construction site supervisor for both Shaw Hotel and Casino, and Chase Confections. You're not to direct what she does. Get that through your—"

"Let's all calm down." Trenton came to his feet and wedged himself between them. His head swung toward Tabitha, then settled on Dominic. "What sort of changes are we talking about?"

Dominic let go another quiet breath to level out and slacken his clenched jaw to avoid cracking a molar. "She marked up the design specs, took out an entire wall, and drew a big, red X on a metal beam to have it removed. We're ten months into construction. Any and all changes must be reviewed and approved by me." His temper roiling just below a simmer, he aimed his glower over his brother's shoulder at the insufferable woman. "It's a support beam; it can't be removed. Valerie tried to tell her that, but she wouldn't listen."

"That ugly pole will get in the way of the refrigerated glass display counter that will sit in its very spot." Stepping around Trenton, she confronted Dominic once more. "I didn't remove the beam. You're making a big deal out of nothing." She looked at Kennedi and Trenton. "I shifted it a measly three feet to the right, is all."

"You. Don't. Get. To. Make. Changes. Without. My. Say." Dominic glared down on her slender build, and damn if he didn't get a swift kick of strawberry-scented shampoo when she whipped that ridiculously long braid back over her shoulder in that way she did, her stark defiance holding firm. Her crinkled brow contorted excruciatingly attractive features that looked ready to slice through a major artery. "The beam stays where it is."

"You don't get to tell me—" she started.

"You heard me, Miss Seils." He pivoted and headed to the door but stopped short when it opened. "Afternoon, Evie." She pushed red-wire frames up the subtle brush of freckles sprinkled across the bridge of her nose, her gaze probing. An easy grin surfaced past his irritation, but not before he saw his anger register in her quizzical stare.

"Dom…uh, hey. You okay?"

Very few times he'd come upon Evie, the third partner in Chase Confections, without her expression carrying a warm smile. Unlike her friend Tabitha. "Good seeing you, Evie. Enjoy your day."

Evie nodded. "Dom, you try to do the same."

He gave a glimpse over his shoulder at Tabitha and met the chill in those hazel eyes that still bored into him like sharp daggers.

"Yeah, I'll try."

"ARGH!" TABITHA SHRILLED and dropped down into the twin armchair opposite Evie. Snatching her sprouts, munching through her fury, she slouched back and gave a look up at Kennedi, with Trenton at her side. "Kenni, who is he to tell us what we can and can't do with our bakery?"

"I see you and Dom went at it again." Evie tore the protective paper off a set of chopsticks and dug into the now-tepid veggie fried rice she'd called ahead for more than a half hour ago. "That explains why he looked ready to explode." Sounding not at all interested, she pointed toward the opposite end of the table. "Someone please pass me a napkin."

Trenton assisted Evie before scooping his suit coat from the couch's armrest and slipping into it. "Tabitha, I believe you've hit a new record with Dom. Rarely have I witnessed my brother at this level of pissed." His head angled to the side, brow lifted. "Quite honestly, I don't think I've ever seen him this enraged…toward a woman, that is. I'll go to the site tomorrow and speak with Valerie to see what can be done about the beam."

Tabitha came to her feet. "Trent, you have a whole team of engineers on site. Why does your brother get to play dictator?"

"He's my COO. I value his input, and I trust he'll see that things get done the way I want them."

"Pain in the ass is what he is." Frustrated, Tabitha jabbed her hands into the back pockets of her denims and paced a narrow path. "Valerie has an issue with me because she has a thing for Dominic. That's what this is really about." She turned to Trenton and Kennedi. "You should see the way the two of them laugh it up, and that woman croons over him. 'Oh, Dominic, you're so funny. That's a nice suit; it fits your frame so perfectly.' Blah, blah blah," she mocked and rolled her eyes. "And he eats that crap up. It's disgusting. So unprofessional. I think Valerie sees me as competition." She dusted her hands and brought them up, palms out. "You can tell her not to worry; he's all hers. Not interested. Self-absorbed pretty boys with an ego chip on their shoulder aren't my type."

With a small smile, Trenton nodded. "You dislike my brother. Duly noted, but I don't think you give him enough credit."

"And I don't think Dom gives Tab enough credit," Kennedi defended her. "She has a right to monitor the construction progress and make decisions that best suit our confectionary."

Tabitha sent a slight appreciative grin her friend's way. "The changes were necessary."

"I'll go talk to him." Trenton turned to Kennedi. "Don't forget to discuss that other matter," he said quietly, and Kennedi nodded.

Tabitha's ears perked up, and Kennedi's gaze brushed Trenton's when his slid her way for the barest of moments. If the two thought they were being cleverly incognito, they'd failed. She'd also caught Kennedi's "subtle" glance at Evie that had been about as conspicuous as her fiancé's a moment ago.

"Thanks for lunch, love." Trenton's arms circled Kennedi's waist and drew her intimately close.

As the couple shared a lingering lip-lock and soft whispers of affection, both Tabitha and Evie directed their concentration to eating their lunch.

Far too much PDA for one o'clock in the afternoon. That said, it was nice to see her friend so happily in love.

"Tabitha, Evie, enjoy your day." Trenton strode out.

When the door closed, her eyes sparkling like rare gemstones and all smiles, Kennedi took a seat on the couch. "Damn, I love that man."

"No, really?" Tabitha delivered her a sardonic grin. "I hadn't noticed."

"I'd never have guessed." Evie snickered.

"Now spill it." With her take-out carton in hand, Tabitha relaxed back in the chair. "I heard what Trenton said. What is it you're supposed to tell me?" Her friend's lovestruck, starry-eyed gaze instantly sobered. Kennedi bit her bottom lip; a telltale sign it wouldn't be anything Tabitha would find pleasant to hear.

"Tab, maybe you should stay away from the construction site for a while."

And there it is. Tabitha cut Kennedi a hard side-eye. "Not a minute ago you agreed that I should be able to monitor our confectionary's construction progress."

"Yes, but—"

"You're taking Dominic's side. Figures," she bristled. "You're engaged to Trenton; it's no shock you'll side with his brother."

"That's not the case and you know it. Stop getting it twisted," Kennedi admonished on a sigh. "Shaw Hotel and Casino is nearly finished. I just don't think changes at this late stage are a good idea. Construction on our confectionary that butts up against the hotel-casino will be completed ahead of schedule. If we start trying to make changes, it'll stretch out our grand opening date. Not to mention, Trenton and I have ads running nonstop all over the place, announcing Chase Confections's grand opening. It's best we don't make any major changes."

"Kenni's right, Tab. Our lease on the temporary space will terminate right around the time we open in the new location. We don't want to have to sign on to another term," Evie added, and both partners supported their appeals with a shared nod. "That said, I'm sure we can figure out a way to work the beam into our décor. I'll get to work on a mural design with our logo to dress it up. But that's not what Kennedi and Trenton were whispering about."

Tabitha looked between her friends, then set her attention on Evie. "That's to say you know what they were whispering about."

Evie turned her head to Kennedi. "Go on, tell her."

Silence. The two stared back at one another, as though trying to will the other to speak.

Kennedi's pencil-stiff posture caused Tabitha to tense tightly herself. "One of you had better start talking before—"

"Okay, okay." Kennedi came to the edge of her seat, her spine as erect as a two-by-four. "Shaw-Vegas's fifth anniversary kicks off next week. The celebration will go on the entire month. There will be celebrity guest appearances, concerts…all sorts of events. Trent thought it would be a good idea to introduce Chase Confections on the West Coast by offering our custom pastries at Shaw's signature restaurant, Pearl Fine Dining."

Evie pinned her frizzy, unruly, dark toffee ringlets behind her ears. "With our bakery reopening soon, we have the East Coast covered. Pearl would be a great promo opportunity to market us out west."

Still bouncing her head back and forth between them, Tabitha laughed. "Why would you think I'd have a problem with that? You two can be so dramatic. West Coast publicity sounds good to me."

"Trent liked the cake design you created for the D.C. casino groundbreaking ceremony last year—so much so, he was hoping you'd do something similar for his Vegas anniversary celebration. Nothing as elaborate as the six-foot Triton," Kennedi clarified. "Trent wants to add a specialty dessert to Pearl's menu, signature crafted like only we can."

Tabitha nodded. "No biggie. We'll bake and ship frozen overnight like we always do."

Kennedi looked at Evie, then back at Tabitha. "We can overnight ship our custom pastries. Baked fresh is what we're known for. But given that it's Shaw's anniversary, we felt you should go to Vegas to put a face to Chase Confections, put us on the West Coast map, so to speak."

"*I* suggested you should go." Evie removed her glasses and buffed the lenses on the end of her T-shirt as she met Tabitha's stare. "Think about it," she said while setting the frames back in place. "When celebrity chefs like Emeril Lagasse, Joël Robuchon, or Wolfgang Puck make an appearance at their restaurants, people crowd in just to get a glimpse at them."

"Evie, I'm not a renowned culinary personality."

"Doesn't matter. Pearl is already booked solid for the

entire month, and that's after only three days of running the Chase Confections promo."

Tabitha blinked. "What promo?" Evie's baby-leaf-green eyes met Kennedi's amber-brown ones, both ladies looking as though they'd been caught with hands in the cookie jar. Tabitha narrowed her own eyes as hard as black ice. "What the hell is going on? What promo?" She directed her glare at Kennedi since she handled their marketing.

"Remember those photos we took of the three of us to promote the bakery relocating to its new home next to Shaw Hotel and Casino? Well, Trent—er, Dominic has it on display at Shaw-Vegas."

"I know you weren't thrilled about how your pics turned out, but it's just a small poster ad, I'm told," Evie hurriedly explained. Squinting, she pinched her fingers close together. "Tiny ad."

Not having to be concerned with the marketing aspect of the business was fine by Tabitha. She trusted Kennedi would see things were done appropriately. Still… "A little heads-up would've been nice."

"Sorry. With running my father's real estate investment firm here on top of managing Chase Confections, I've been crazy busy. As Evie said, the ad has been up only three days. It's getting a lot of buzz. It's actually pretty popular. Even our website has picked up double the traffic."

"All the more reason you should go to Vegas," Evie added.

As Tabitha sipped her bottled water, she caught their shared side-eye glances woven within a silent exchange, reading the undercurrent of their agenda. "How about you just say what this is really about. You're trying to keep me from the Wharf construction site, get me as far away from D.C. as possible. I see you two have it all worked out. Kennedi, I guess you were just pretending to have my back earlier. So much for partnership. Sistahood. You two plotting behind my—"

"Tab, it's not like that at all." Evie quickly sat forward. "Kennedi was hesitant to bring up Vegas because when we tell you Dominic will be there as well, we felt you'd say—"

"I'd say oh hell no!" Tabitha scowled and shook her head in stark protest. "Damn right. Count me out if he's involved."

Evie threw her hands up. "See, we knew you'd react this way."

"Tabitha, Dom is Shaw Enterprise's COO. Of course he'll oversee all things relating to Shaw's—both D.C. and Vegas." Kennedi let go a soft sigh. "Come on, you can tolerate the guy for one week."

"Right?" Evie tagged on. "You'll be working in the restaurant and likely too busy to even notice him. I'm sure he'll be just as preoccupied with his duties. Tab, it's for our business. You want us to grow, don't you?"

Of course Tabitha wanted the business to thrive. Featuring their desserts at Pearl would aid that path. And it was Vegas. Spending a week, albeit for work, wouldn't be half bad. But a week with Dominic Balaska's bossy ass? *Ugh.* It set her enthusiasm very low. That said, this was about business, and these ladies would do just about anything for her. "Fine, I'll go. But if that man thinks he's going to control what I do out there—"

"I'm sure he won't," Evie hurried to say. "Now, what are you wearing on your date tomorrow night?"

"Date?" Kennedi's eyes widened. "You have a date tomorrow and didn't tell me?" She directed her surprise at Evie, her brow pinched as she pushed back against the couch. "Evidently, you're in the know. I guess I've been placed outside the sista circle?"

"You're being ridiculous." Finishing off her sprouts, Tabitha mumbled around her last bite, "It's not a big deal. It's just a guy Troy knows. My brother's been pressuring me to start dating again. I mentioned it to Evie two nights ago while we were working late at the boutique. You've been busy here at Chase Investments, not to mention sleeping mostly at Trent's place lately. Kenni, this is the first time I've seen you all week."

"Actually, Trent wants me to move in with him. As you said, I'm there most nights anyway."

Tabitha had expected Kennedi and Trenton would cohabitate at some point. She'd done it herself with her chickenshit of an ex-fiancé, Jeffrey.

There was no question Trenton Shaw, the hotel and casino mogul, loved her best friend. It was also safe to say Kennedi wouldn't end up on the receiving end of a breakup three days before her wedding and subsequently suffer through a miscarriage. *Memories.*

She'd moved in with Kennedi a little more than a year ago, soon after that hellish nightmare. It'd been a godsend to have her friend there during that dark time for support.

"We may as well discuss it now. When will you be moving out?" Tabitha asked.

"I wanted to talk to you about buying my house." Kennedi gave her a tentative look. "What do you think?"

"You already know I don't have the funds to buy a doll-house right now let alone your home. Until the store reopens in its new location and starts to draw in a strong revenue stream, that won't happen."

"I didn't mean you'd have to purchase it this minute. We can write something up that spells out the plan toward ownership, one that fits within your timetable. Speaking of dollhouse, how's the Headley project coming along? Were you able to set the gum paste in the curve shape for the shingles without them cracking?"

"Evie and I finished the roof this morning, and she was able to get all of the furniture pieces done."

"Yes, we should be able to complete the project by to-morrow. Then we'll start on the baby cradle for the Masons' gender reveal party." Evie beamed. "I can't wait."

"I'll come by the boutique to help you two after I check in on my father at Brighton Gardens. The new medication he's taking has helped with the seizures."

"That's great to hear." Tabitha reached over and took hold of her friend's hand, giving a light squeeze. Evie clasped the other. With Kennedi's father suffering with a brain tumor that triggered dementia, Kennedi had been running his company, Chase Investments, for the past year as well as putting in her time at the bakery boutique. She'd been juggling quite a lot of plates.

"Evie and I have things covered. Kenni, you go see your father and spend time with your fiancé. I'll—" Cut off by her cell phone ring, Tabitha dug it out from where it had wedged in the chair's side cushion and checked the display. She sucked in a low breath but tried to mask it around a light cough. Heart beating like a drum against her breastbone, she kept her expression blank and bald-faced lied to her friends.

"It's Troy. He probably wants to tell me not to cancel this blind date he's concocted." The ringing stopped and the phone prompted a voicemail message. "I'd better get back to the boutique." She pushed up out of the chair.

"Wait. This blind date, what do you know about the guy? What's his name? His profession?" Kennedi asked.

"Well, Mom," Tabitha teased, "his name's Randall Cuff. He has a small business… I think it's remodeling or something."

"I told her to check him out," Evie remarked. "Troy's your brother. I'm sure he made certain Randall isn't some weirdo. But still, Tab, you should look the guy up. These days you can't be too careful."

Tabitha shrugged. It wasn't like there would be a second date. Men. She didn't need the headache. "Randall did some roof work at Troy's house."

"Okay, and?" Kennedi nodded, her stare direct.

"Kenni, that's exactly what I said, so I stalked his social media." Evie got up from the chair and plucked her phone from her purse on the side table, then plopped down on the couch. With their heads angled close, she and Kennedi scrolled through a host of photos. "Here he is."

"He has that Theo James sort of vibe." Kennedi zoomed the pictures in and out.

"Yes, I can see that," Evie agreed.

"Theo who?" Tabitha sat beside Evie to get a glimpse of the guy. Dark brown hair, rich brown eyes, nice tan—he looked decent enough, though she wasn't into the around-the-clock, five-o'clock shadow kind of beard.

"Theo James. You know, from that movie, *Divergent*." Evie did an internet search for Tabitha's benefit, showed her a photo of the actor, then switched back to Randall's Face-book spread. "Ooh, that's a really nice boat. You think it's his?"

Tabitha took the phone and swiped through a couple of pics of Randall and his boat out on the open water. "He's all right, I guess."

"But he's no Dominic Balaska." Evie grinned.

"That's a good thing." She handed back the phone then came to her feet.

"Come on, Tab, don't front. You can admit Dom's hot. I don't believe I've ever seen eyes as blue as his. I wonder if they're colored contacts?"

Tabitha grabbed her purse from the armchair and draped the black leather strap over her head to rest on her shoulder. "And I've never known a bigger pain in the ass."

"But it's a really nice ass."

"Evie!" Tabitha gaped.

"What? Quite honestly, I haven't had sex in nearly two years. I'm able to spot a shapely ass on a mannequin."

Looking at one another, they all burst into a roil of laughter. Tabitha could relate; she was riding somewhat close to that same wave of abstinence herself.

"Evie, sounds like it's you who has the hots for Balaska."

"Not at all. It's merely an observation. Clearly Dominic

is into you. Besides, I'm still dealing with Patrick's bullshit. I definitely wouldn't want to drag some poor soul into my little house of Patrick horrors."

"Girl, stop." Kennedi snorted a laugh. "You're going through a divorce; you're not dead."

"Tell her." Tabitha nodded.

"I suppose you're right." Evie turned back to Tabitha. "As I was saying, the way you and Dom butt heads demonstrates you two have a connection. I was right about Kennedi and Trenton, wasn't I? Those two were always arguing, complete adversaries. Now they're engaged."

"I wouldn't say complete adversaries," Kennedi murmured with a sheepish grin.

Tabitha rolled her eyes. *What an absurdity.* "Your study is flawed. If you recall, Kennedi and Trenton had sex in the kitchen of our bakery when they were practically at each other's throats. Rest assured that'll never happen with Dominic and me."

"Kennedi and Trenton were a sexually charged pair for sure. And never say never, girlfriend. They proved my point."

Tabitha sighed deeply. Evie had a psychology degree, number two of three. The woman was a walking textbook. Her parents had nearly disowned her when she'd decided to drop her Ivy League track for culinary school. But her friend was way off the mark on this one. This was psychoanalysis bull crap.

Offering a small smile, she started toward the door. "Kennedi, give your father a hug for me."

"I will."

"Wait." Evie followed her. "I took a Lyft to get here. I'll ride back with you."

"No!" Tabitha spun and threw a hand up like a guard at a crosswalk, stopping Evie dead in her tracks. Catching their peculiar stares—not ready to say where she was really headed—she let another lie fly. "I need to hop over to see Troy to get the four-one-one on this Randall Cuff guy. Like you said, I should find out more about him. I'll see you back at the boutique later." She turned away, then pivoted back and handed Evie her car keys while pulling open the door, one foot straddling the threshold. "I'll catch a Lyft. Troy's likely at work. Trying to find parking on the street by the firehouse can be such a pain."

"You're sure?"

"Yep. The car's in the garage next door, second level near the stairs. Hugs, ladies."

On the way down in the elevator, she quickly ordered her ride, then listened to the voicemail message:

Good afternoon, Miss Seils. It's Marylin Winslow at Parker Adoption Agency. I'd like to talk to you about a client who may be of interest to you. I know it's short notice, but if you're able to stop by the office today, I can provide more details. Hope to hear from you.

A barrel of nerves stalled the air in Tabitha's chest.

Wow!

Chapter Two

"GIRL OR BOY?" Tabitha studied every angle of the ultrasound image to try to determine the sex, then delivered a broad smile to Ms. Winslow across the desk. "I can't tell." She'd read all the books and researched every website she could find on adoption. A private organization, Parker Adoption Agency had successfully placed more than seventy-five hundred children in its twenty-three-year history.

"Girl." Ms. Winslow slid the file across the desk. "The mother, Kaitlyn, is seventeen, Caucasian. She's four months along. The father, Oscar, also seventeen, is African American. Kaitlyn's parents are recently divorced, but they want her to finish high school and go to college, and Oscar's family want the same for him."

"Both were involved in the decision to place the child for adoption?"

"Yes, the young parents signed the papers together. They're from Shelby, Indiana, but Kaitlyn and her mother moved to West Virginia. The family doesn't have much money. In addition to the legal fees, Kaitlyn is including her medical expenses in the adoption contract. This will increase the total cost of the package I initially quoted you. Kaitlyn's request is that the child be placed with a family of mixed race. She feels it will benefit the little one. I immediately thought of you as one of the possible candidates."

Biracial herself, but with parents whose ethnicity were the opposite of Kaitlyn and Oscar, Tabitha understood Kaitlyn's concern. Teaching the child to embrace her whole self at a young age would be paramount.

Three, maybe even four children had been her plan. She was pushing twenty-nine in just shy of three months; her friends would say she had plenty of time to meet the right guy, get married, and have a baby. It didn't necessarily have to be in that order. She wasn't picky. But for others, time ran slower than it did for her. She ate clean, got in a workout at a minimum of four days a week, never smoked, enjoyed a drink or two but never over-imbibed, and yet she could almost guarantee she'd never get pregnant. *There's always hope*, her oncologist had said. But after losing one ovary to cancer and scraping the other one raw of the vile, soul-crushing disease, hope had been in short supply.

Yet she'd beaten the odds for eleven weeks and four days.

Nearly three months along, it still didn't feel real, as if the unexpected gift had been granted to someone else instead of her. Tabitha pressed a hand to her stomach, choked with joy as she studied what looked to be no more than a smudge on the image.

Tacking the ultrasound photo beneath the ladybug magnet on the fridge, she laughed, a happy chirping sound. She'd been riding the happiness and excitement train the entire day.

She set two place settings on the dining table and crossed back into the kitchen just as the entry door squeaked on its hinges. The distinct clink of the latch followed. Moments later,

Jeffrey stood across the space of the kitchen. Clean-shaven head, distinguishingly angular nose, soft jawbone structure—he wouldn't be labeled handsome in the conventional sense. But it was his intellect that appealed the most to her.

"Jeez, babe, look at you." Sweat beaded his forehead. Moisture ringed the armpits of his pale blue button-down. No surprise. Temperatures in the DMV had been hovering around ninety degrees by midday. D.C., Maryland, and Virginia residents played roulette when dressing on any given day. Jeff's two-block walk to the parking garage from his office could have him drenched in under five minutes. But it was also tax season. He tended to perspire in stressful situations. A corporate CPA for one of the biggest D.C. firms, he had quite a lot to contend with on a daily basis. To add to it, he'd been trying to make partner for nearly six months.

Tabitha quickly poured and handed him a glass of crisp Pinot Grigio. "Go take a shower and relax. Dinner's almost ready."

"I want us to talk."

"It can wait." She'd start with her day and he'd finish with his. That was their routine. "Go rest a bit first."

"We need to talk. There are some things I have to say." He swept a hand down his face and set weary, brown eyes upon her.

"Then at least sit before you fall down. You look wiped out."

She pulled the pork tenderloin from the oven and basted while starting in on the events of the day. "The store was a madhouse this afternoon. There were two buses of middle schoolers returning from a Lincoln Memorial field trip. They nearly wiped out today's inventory. Kennedi, Evie, and I had to bake an entire—"

"I can't do it."

"Can't do what?" At the stove, she gave a look over her shoulder. He was still standing at the bridge of the kitchen and family room, the wine she'd given him untouched.

"I thought I could, but I can't. I'm not ready for all of this. First it was the cancer. Then a baby. Now a wedding." He shook his head. "I'm in line to become junior partner. A wedding and a kid, it's a lot on me right now. I can't do it."

She turned to face him, the two-ton anvil of pressure that weighed down on her chest making it difficult to breathe. "I didn't ask to get cancer, Jeff."

"That's not what I meant."

"Then what do you mean? Our wedding is in three days. Everything's set. My nana flew in from Seattle. She's eighty-four with arthritis. Do you know how difficult that was for her?"

"I know." His voice was weak. He let go a heavy breath and ran both hands over his glistening crown, linking them at the back of his neck, dark eyes angled toward the floor. "I was with someone. I didn't mean for it to happen."

Tabitha blinked. There was no way she'd heard him correctly. The bells were ringing much too loudly between her ears. "You didn't just say what I think you said." Silence. "Damn it, Jeff, look at me!"

His head snapped up. "Everything started moving so fast— the baby, the wedding plans, you moving in—"

"You asked—no, practically begged me for months to move in here!" Her voice revved. "I sold my townhouse, and took a loss I might add, because you didn't want to live there, said it was too small."

"It was. And my place is closer to my office."

"By only fifteen minutes, and it's farther away from my bakery. Who is she?"

"It was a mistake. I'm sorry. I don't want to hurt you. I'm just not ready for all of this."

Eyes blurred from the flash of tears, she felt sick. Literally felt the bile's slow crawl into her throat, feeling as though she was caught in some tragic, horrific nightmare. "You're sorry. What…" She swallowed hard, but the pressure in her chest wouldn't give way. "You screw around on me and then say you're sorry. What the hell am I supposed to do with that?"

"I don't want to hurt you," he repeated. "I've booked a hotel until we figure out the living arrangements."

"You're kicking me out is what you're saying. That's what you're doing. Be a man and say it, damn it!" she raged with an aggressive step forward, fist squeezed tight at her sides. He flinched and threw a hand up. "Jeff, I want to hear you say the words!"

"You should calm down. Think about the baby."

She gaped. The audacity. "Are you seriously going to try to go there? You weren't thinking about the baby when you were screwing around on me!"

"I should go." His eyes darted down to her tightly closed fists, then came up as he took several slow steps back like prey confronting a viper, before hurrying out.

She turned her head to the image on the fridge as pulsing spasms roiled low in her stomach, turning over and over. The pain struck sharp, the sudden throb seizing tight with debilitating pressure, throwing her into an agonizing crouch. "Jeff?" The sound of her voice came out in a whispered breath of agony. A touch at the wetness between her thighs revealed what she'd feared as blood streamed down her legs, staining her pristine white sneakers—

"Miss Seils?"

Tabitha looked down at her hand pressed to her stomach where the ache of her loss had been so excruciatingly devastating and where Ms. Winslow's large, green eyes sat pinned, unblinking. She straightened in the chair and dropped her hand to her side, shutting out the horrific memory before it overwhelmed her. "I'm sorry, could you repeat that?"

"I said Kaitlyn will want to interview you as well as the other two couples."

Couples. Being a village of one might be a problem. For a mere millisecond, she thought of Randall Cuff, a man she had yet to meet, as someone who might suit long-term. "I suppose Kaitlyn's looking for the traditional set?"

Ms. Winslow entwined her slender, pale fingers upon the desk. "Parker Adoption doesn't discriminate. We've been very successful placing children in single-family households. It's more important to us that the child gets a stable, loving home. It's what Kaitlyn wants for her daughter. I presented several profiles for her to review. She was very specific in what she was looking for: young, educated, and financially capable. I showed her your profile but explained, however, that you'd only recently inquired and that we're in the beginning stage of the screening process. I don't typically share a candidate with the mother until all of the boxes are checked, but I got a good feeling about you at our first meeting." Ms. Winslow glanced down at the folder in front of her. "We'll have to perform the home inspection, and there are still interviews needed with your family along with your two business partners. I'll need contact numbers."

Tabitha winced. "I see." A conversation with her family

as well as Kennedi and Evie would need to happen fast.

"Miss Seils—"

"Please call me Tabitha."

Ms. Winslow smiled lightly. "Tabitha, I know this is quite sudden. And together with the additional medical expenses, it can become steep. We always say to try to plan for unexpected expenses. If you'd prefer to wait, it's understandable. There will be another opportunity."

Two years or even longer was the realistic timetable she'd been told to expect when a newborn would become available.

"Should we proceed?" Ms. Winslow asked.

Tabitha's stomach somersaulted. "Yes."

"All right. I'll need you to complete these forms. We'll also need the first installment following final review of your file. The fees and anticipated medical expenses are spelled out here." Shuffling a few papers, she handed over several.

Tabitha tried to keep her expression from betraying her shock. "Thirty-five thousand, eight hundred, sixty-six is the first installment?"

"Yes. Complete the bottom portion and sign. It will authorize the wire transfer. You'll note the next installment is due at the end of the second trimester, with a final payment at the birth of the little one...before the child is handed over to you."

Thirty-five thousand, eight hundred, sixty-six. It was a substantial chunk of money. Tabitha had enough for only the first installment. She hadn't expected to hear from the adoption agency for about a year, which would've given her time to save. By then the bakery would be up and running in its new location. Business was sure to skyrocket, especially now that Chase Confections had an in with Shaw Hotel and Casino. And introducing their desserts at the Pearl restaurant in Vegas would help to boost business. So, yes, there would be a strong revenue stream flowing her way. But nearly a hundred grand due sooner than later should Kaitlyn choose her? That stood to be a problem.

She could almost feel the baby's light weight cradled in her arms. She'd stroke her tiny hand and downy hair. She'd soothe her cries with soft coos and sweet words. Day and night would become one continuous circle, the baby turning her into a walking zombie when she found it impossible to sleep. But she'd get one of those carriers, the kind worn close to the chest to keep her little one calmed by the rhythm of her heartbeat.

No doubt her life would be forever changed, and Tabitha welcomed all that came with being a mom. This was her chance. Perhaps her only chance. She couldn't turn away the opportunity to have what she'd so desperately yearned for.

As she filled out the initial form, she wondered how Kennedi and Evie would react to her plans to adopt. Her parents would surely try to talk her out of it. Her girlfriends were ride or die, but there was that slim chance they'd object as well. Right now, she didn't want to hear any dissuading arguments.

Her cell phone chimed a text.

Troy: Don't ghost on Randall tomorrow night. I mean it, Tabby!

Born seven minutes earlier, he didn't hesitate to remind her who was the oldest.

She handed back the papers and fanned through the

twenty or so on her lap. "I'll complete the rest of the forms tonight and get them back to you."

Ms. Winslow gave a quick scan of the document. "I think everything's in order for now." They both stood. "I'll be in touch."

"Thank you."

A single mom working long hours? Women did it all the time. *I got this.*

Chapter Three

"I NEED TO take this." Dominic untangled his date's arm from his, slid out of the booth, and headed toward the rear of the restaurant.

"Trent, hey."

"Evening. You have a minute?"

"Yeah, what's up?" He planted himself close to the knotty pine paneled wall to get out of the way of the busy foot traffic of those moving to and from the bathroom facilities.

"As you know, I'll be headed to Dubai and will be there for about three weeks. We'll soon have all of the investors in play. If all goes as planned, we could break ground on the Dubai condo project by fall of this year."

"Which means you won't make it to Vegas for any of the anniversary celebration."

"Afraid not."

"On the condo project, I wanted to talk to you about that. I'd like to put my name in the mix. The minimum footprint, twenty mil."

"Oh yeah? Do you have money I don't know about hidden in your mattress, or have you satisfied your trust clause? Who's the lucky lady? Because until that happens, it's about the only way you'll see any of those funds."

"I'm aware. You let me worry about that." A short distance down the narrow hallway, he spotted Tabitha Seils exiting the ladies' room. With her phone at her ear, head hanging low, she turned toward the wall. Was she distressed? He moved closer and caught terse clips of her conversation. Some Randall dude was about to get ghosted. *I'll be damned.* The woman was planning to skip out on her companion.

"If you can come up with the minimum, you're in. Dom? Hey, you're there?"

"Yes, I'll check in with you tomorrow. Gotta go." He disconnected and crossed the corridor just as Tabitha ended her call, pivoted, and slammed smack into his chest. Her phone hit the polished tile floor with a resounding crash. They both bent to retrieve it, but he was a bit faster on the grab. The screen had shattered into a multitude of spider-web-like fissures.

"Shit," she hissed.

"You do realize Apple has come out with at least three, maybe even four versions since that one."

She looked up. Surprise registered in her eyes, then her gaze narrowed. "Balaska, what are you doing here?" They pinned themselves close to the wall to get out of the way of passersby.

"Well, Miss Seils, seeing as it's a restaurant, one typically visits the establishment to eat."

"You broke my phone."

"On the contrary, you practically mowed me down." He'd hardly even stumbled. Slipping his hands into the front pockets of his slacks, he rested a shoulder against the wall and gestured with a nod across the space. "I was taking a call and saw you huddled over here. Thought you might be ill and in need of assistance until I realized what was actually going down."

"Going down?"

"Do you know how difficult it is to get a reservation here?"

"I see you managed it," she sneered. "What's your point?"

"I know the executive chef. It's never an issue for me. As for your date, if he doesn't have connections as I do, I'm betting he had to put up some serious stack." He rubbed the tips of his fingers together. "You know what I mean?"

She rolled her eyes. "I'm aware of what it means. Again, what's your point?"

"The guy probably did major planning to dine here. Damn shame that you'd bail on him like this."

She frowned. "Is that your thing, peeping in on others' conversations?"

"You'd like to think so, but it wasn't my intention. Like I said, I initially thought you were in distress." Dominic's attention momentarily shifted to a tall, leggy brunette who subtly winked at him on her strut past. He looked back at Tabitha. Her eyes, those remarkable eyes, were vivid and full of condemnation.

"Typical." Her lips curled, like she'd tasted something foul.

He took offense, though he didn't have the right. Still… "You should've saved your date the trouble by not showing up at all. And here I thought you were only frosty toward me. Yes, put the unfortunate man you're here with out of his misery. Good evening, Miss Seils."

HIS WORDS WERE cold, and his small grin was clearly mocking. As he strode away in no particular hurry, heat slid up into Tabitha's cheeks. But he was right about one thing. Dabney's was Michelin-starred. Unless you were one of D.C.'s finest, it was damn near impossible to score a table here.

She'd hardly gone beyond lip gloss in her prep for this date. The fact that Dominic Balaska could dissect and discern her so easily pissed her off. But more upsetting, his criticism cut core-deep, coiled and squeezed tight.

Who the hell does he thinks he is to judge me? The man knew nothing about her. He didn't warrant the tightness in her chest.

She made her way back to the table just as Randall started to rise from his chair, his brown eyes concerned.

"There you are. Are you okay? You were gone for quite some time. I was about to come check on you."

Tabitha tried to respond but had to clear the clawing strain in her throat to halt the tears threatening to crest. The fact that Balaska was the cause upset her all the more.

"There was a long line." She brought up her menu and gave it a quick scan, mainly to block out Randall's scrutiny. He'd been in the middle of a story about a drywall incident when she'd excused herself. Hopefully, he wouldn't continue.

"Ah, of course. Well, your absence gave me time to decide on the grilled halibut."

The waiter approached the table and set a glass of Chardonnay before Tabitha, then jotted down their orders.

"I took the liberty of ordering you a glass of wine," Randall said.

Typical man, always assuming he knew what a woman wanted. Her first glass had been Cîroc with a splash of cranberry juice. That should've been his first clue.

Ugh. Misdirected irritation at its finest. She had to give the guy credit for making an effort.

With her glass tipped to her mouth, she lifted her gaze above the rim and caught sight of Dominic seated in a corner booth. His unblinking gaze held solidly on her for a long moment, his face a blank mask. On a slow shutter of his eyes, he turned those icy blues to the porcelain, blonde woman hemmed in close beside him, practically seated in his lap—attractive, in an overdone makeup sort of way. She took note of the woman's pretty, spaghetti-strap coral dress, and those perfect boobs that practically spilled out of the severely low-cut bodice. Tabitha slid her gaze back to Dominic and once again found his eyes on her. Was he waiting to see if she'd bail? She wouldn't give the pompous pain in the ass the satisfaction. *Damn him and his dark hair styled just right, perfectly golden-tanned features, and well-coordinated and impeccably fitted tone-on-tone, charcoal-gray getup.* Aside from his stuck-up, no-it-all attitude, there wasn't anything she could find to criticize.

Turning her attention to Randall, half listening to him drone on about his work, she smiled and nodded where she deemed appropriate. He was nice enough, but there simply wasn't a spark on her end.

Tabitha came to her feet, cutting short Randall's anecdotal ramble. "I see an old friend. Mind if we join them?"

"Uh—"

Not waiting for Randall to return from his sudden stupor to agree or object, she stopped their waiter and asked to have their meals brought to the corner booth, then headed across the crowded dining room and came to stand before the couple's table.

"Dominic Balaska, isn't this a surprise."

He looked up from his date. "I—"

"It's Tabitha." She planted a hand on her hip, laying it on thick. "Have I changed that much that you don't recognize me? Wow, how long has it been? Two…maybe three years, right? Come here." Painting on a broad smile, she stretched her arms wide.

With a wary look blanketing his features, he slid out of the booth and stepped into her tight embrace. "Woman, what are you up to?" he muttered in her ear.

"I'm a cold bitch, huh?" she whispered back, then drew away, framing her face with a cool smile.

"That's not what I meant." He hadn't bothered to whisper, and it brought about peculiar looks from their companions.

Tabitha knew precisely what he'd meant when he'd called her frosty. The chary expression he now wore should've been enough payback for his damn insulting comment earlier, but she wasn't done. She extended her hand to his date. "Hi, I'm Tabitha Seils. Hope it's okay that I interrupted your evening. I saw Dom over here." She shot him a well-stretched smile. "We go way back."

"Celeste Finley. Nice to meet you."

"Celeste, is it okay if we join you? I'd love to catch up with Dominic. It feels like forever since we've seen one another. You don't mind do you, Dom?"

He stood there staring at her through ticking seconds, then gave her a narrowed side look before sticking out his hand to her date. "Dominic Balaska."

"Randall Cuff."

"Excuse me, everyone."

Their heads whirled toward the two waiters who held their orders. Tabitha turned back to the group with a sly grin. "I made a presumption." She smiled at Celeste and shot a thumb over at Dominic. "I remember how he likes to party, that one. The more the merrier, right?" She sat down and scooted over for Randall, who quite frankly looked disappointed that their intimate evening for two had turned into a gathering of four.

"How did you two meet?" Celeste directed her question to Dominic after the wine had been served and they'd settled in with their meals.

"Allow me." Tabitha sat forward, taking delight in her desire to show the woman Dominic's true colors. "I'm part owner of a bakery that Dom—" She paused, startled by his reach across the table. Warm fingers curled around hers. His thumb brushed back and forth across her knuckles in the gentlest of motions, rasping small slivers of sensation that hummed throughout her entire body. She jerked her hand free.

"No, let me tell it, Tabby." The grin he flashed at her

was downright wolfish before he looked at their dates. "Tabby. That's what I used to call her. Anyway, I was once heavily involved with animal rescue and even took in a few strays but had to give it all up. Tabitha is severely allergic. She demanded that they go away. The dander, you see."

"That was so kind of you. To be forced to give up something you loved doing had to be difficult. I love animals. All sorts," starry-eyed Celeste crooned, and Tabitha fought not to roll her eyes.

The man didn't stutter a single syllable. Lies apparently flowed from him about as naturally as breathing. "What are you talking about? That's not what—"

"You're right." Dominic's lips turned up slightly with his gaze holding hers across the table. "It's not the part of the story that's nearly as interesting. Like Tab mentioned," he said, using her nickname with friendly familiarity, "she owns a specialty bakery boutique." He winked. "One night after leaving the shelter, I stopped at her store just before closing for something to conquer my sweet tooth. There were these miniature chocolate cupcakes in the display case. I asked for a half dozen. As the cashier started packaging my order, I popped one into my mouth." His eyes closed, and he licked his noticeably smooth lips. "Melt in your mouth. If you haven't tried her desserts, you're missing out. I have yet to taste anything better."

"I *have* had the pleasure and can agree her desserts are delicious," Randall asserted. With his gaze holding hers, he took Tabitha's hand in his and planted a kiss upon the back of it. "When my crew and I were working on your brother's roof, he kept a box of Chase Confections on hand for us.

Your blackberry and vanilla glazed cheese Danish is like nothing I've ever tasted. Remarkable." He delivered another light kissed across her knuckles.

Dominic's brow suddenly drew down, his head tilted, and his eyes zeroed in on her and Randall's linked hands. His stare lifted and held hers in an almost harsh, silent command. She found herself pulling her hand free of Randall's. The action seemed to break Dominic's severe mien, yet those glacial blues felt all-consuming, dominating, as he watched her over the rim of his glass.

"You two met at her store. Got it," Randall drawled and forked a piece of his halibut, conveying mediocre interest.

"Yes, we did, but not yet," Dominic said. "The cupcake had peanut butter filling. I didn't read the label. I have a peanut allergy. Instantly, my throat closed up on me, and I was without my EpiPen. I collapsed right there in the store."

"No!" Celeste shrieked and pressed a hand to her generously exposed cleavage, riveted by the man's *tall* tale. "What happened?"

Tabitha had to admit, she, too, had become drawn into Dominic's well-crafted story and wanted to know how it ended.

"I woke sprawled out on the floor with Miss Seils there performing CPR on me before the paramedics arrived." He looked at her. "She saved my life. In a way, you could also say it was our first kiss. Right, Tabby?" He winked and moistened his lips.

A strange quivering stirred in Tabitha's belly. What would those smooth lips feel like pressed against hers? And he'd in essence shaped her as the champion in his widely stretched fib. Since he'd hijacked her plan to humiliate him, she stuffed her mouth with grilled asparagus, unsure what to make of the man.

"Evidently, things ended between you two. May I ask, how long was the relationship?" Randall questioned.

"Yes," Celeste added and snaked her arm in a possessive curl around Dominic's bulky bicep.

"Not long," Tabitha blurted, taking note of the woman's *bitch, back the fuck up, he's mine* smoke signal.

"She broke up with me," Dominic came back, seeming unaware or simply unconcerned that his date looked bothered.

"We wanted different things," Tabitha returned and smiled at Celeste. "His attention tended to drift elsewhere."

"The blame can be shared." Dominic's smooth voice dropped a register. "I think we didn't take the time to really get to know one another." Their gazes held as tense silence hung for an awkward moment before he turned to his date and smiled, bringing her back into his sphere. "But all's for the best."

Okay, what just happened? Tabitha felt as though they'd crossed over from pretense into something else for a moment, of which she wasn't quite sure.

The rest of the evening, Dominic showered Celeste with attention in between cracking jokes that had the woman falling into breast-jiggling laughter. He even managed to get Randall to loosen up and laugh at his arid humor now and again.

Tabitha found herself watching Dominic's every move, the way a dimple formed in his left cheek when he'd smile with a genuine swell of humor. How his dark lashes were exceptionally long for a man. And the guy's stare was forever intense; the entire night she found herself drowning in the sea of his gaze. She hadn't paid much attention before, but Evie had been right. *Does he wear colored contacts?* His eyes were unnaturally blue—dark pupils surrounded by glaciers of blue fire. She blinked. *Blue fire? Where the hell did that come from?* She dropped her gaze from him and centered on her tiramisu but not before his attention shifted and he caught her gawking.

"You could do better."

Tabitha jerked her head up from her plate to Dominic, then over at Randall, who was heavily indulging in his raspberry cheesecake. "That's a rud—"

"The tiramisu." Dominic nodded at her dessert; he'd ordered the same. "No doubt it would taste better if you'd had a hand in it." His telling eyes slid to Randall then back to her as he pushed his plate away. "Too soft."

"I've had worse."

Conceding with a nod, he returned his full attention to Celeste. The woman seemed to literally brighten like Christmas lights, lapping up his affection. Tabitha could see why. Dominic was completely zoned into his date, refilling Celeste's wineglass at the precise moment needed. He pulled off his suit jacket and draped Celeste's shoulders when she complained about a chill in the air. He held her hand and caressed the back of it in that familiar, slow stroking when he spoke to her and only her.

Goodness, to be doted on like that. An irrational undercurrent of jealousy constricted in Tabitha's chest as she forced down every bit of the too-soft, too-sweet dessert. First Valerie and now Celeste. Was this how he treated women—shower with attention and affection, get what he wanted, then off to the next one? She couldn't decide which upset her more: the fact that he was a womanizer or that he showed no interest in her. Well, there was that short stint when they'd first met nearly a year ago. He'd put out clear signs, but she'd shut him down.

About two hours later, standing outside the restaurant, Randall handed the valet his ticket, and Tabitha did the same. She'd driven herself in case she needed to cut out early and would have done just that if it hadn't been for Dominic. He'd insisted she and Randall hang around as he ordered another bottle of wine and kept the table animated with surprisingly pleasant conversation. Tabitha discovered he liked art history, as did she. They all touched on politics and shared music taste. He talked about the theater—Broadway plays, not your local cinema. Another shared interest.

Within mere seconds of them stepping curbside, a shimmery black, Audi R8 Spyder drop-top rolled up. The valet exited the sleek vehicle and handed Dominic the key fob. Having a brother who'd been fixated on cars his entire life, Tabitha had picked up a thing or two. That badass ride easily cost a good six figures.

With Celeste hanging on his arm as she had been the entire night, Dominic approached. "Glad we could catch up. This was fun."

For the most part, Tabitha couldn't disagree but didn't let on. "I suppose."

The valet pulled to the curb in a midnight-blue Range

Rover and handed Randall his key fob. Behind it, another attendant came to a stop in Tabitha's ruby-red Kia Sportage.

Randall turned to her. "This was…well, an interesting evening to say the least. Sharing a first date with an ex-boyfriend is a new one for me. Glad you two could catch up."

Ex-boyfriend. *Not even close.*

Tabitha initiated a hug to cut through the awkwardness. Clearly, Randall wouldn't ask her out again. "Have a good night." What else could she say? He delivered a handshake to Dominic and Celeste, then went on his way.

She turned back to the pair. "Celeste, it was nice meeting you. Thanks for letting me crash your evening." All things considered, there wasn't anything negative to say about the woman. Tabitha wondered if she would've been as accommodating as Celeste if an *ex-girlfriend* had commandeered her date?

Hell no!

"No worries. Dominic and I have the rest of the night," Celeste returned, wearing a suggestive grin while clinging as tight as Saran Wrap to the man. "I'll have to come by your bakery to see if Dominic's rave about your desserts isn't exaggerated."

A small jab, but Tabitha didn't take offense. In fact, she couldn't control the claw of envy that had been scratching at her all damn night. "You do that."

She looked on as Dominic settled Celeste into his passenger seat, then he turned back to her. Before she could deliver him a cordial farewell, he pulled her into a full-bodied hug, strong arms circling her frame, a tight breasts-to-chest intimate embrace. She turned her nose into his neck to take in the intoxicating scent of his cologne, not sure what provoked that spontaneous action but unable to help it.

He drew back. His eyes dipped to her lips for a long moment, and dear sweet jeez, his head tilted in that kissable angle as he leaned in, his trajectory in direct aim of her mouth. Her lips parted slightly in welcome invitation, but he veered. Exceptionally smooth lips caught her cheek. "I think we're even," he whispered at her ear, a brushstroke of his warm breath fanning her neck. "Good night, Miss Seils."

She came out of his warm embrace and felt an immediate chill. "Don't you mean Tabby?" Keeping up a strong front, contrary to her rapidly racing pulse, she climbed into her idling car, feeling as though the earth had twisted on its axis, the air around her suddenly stifling. Dominic Balaska had somehow left her craving his kiss.

Chapter Four

CHASE CONFECTIONS WAS smack in the middle of its weekend morning rush.

Tabitha made her way behind the glass counter where the cashiers, Amy and Portia, had things under control. Ronny, with Carlos—who'd graduated from culinary school last spring and who Tabitha was mentoring in custom cake design—were busy packaging up the orders as fast as Amy and Portia called them out.

"Morning, everyone. Where's Evie?" Their manager typically assisted the employees in the storefront during crunch time.

"Some guy came by," Amy answered while maneuvering around Tabitha to pour up a large coffee for the patron standing before her register.

"What guy?" Tabitha stepped back to get out of the way when Amy doubled back.

"Dunno." Portia skirted past her and grabbed a box of cinnamon scones from Carlos. "They're in back."

The small corner property was a temporary home for Chase Confections while they awaited the new store opening on the D.C. Wharf. The original bakery location had been Kennedi's mother's for more than thirty years before it'd been demolished to build a parking garage for Shaw Hotel and Casino. Kennedi fought against Trenton Shaw to try to save her family's legacy. The pair made a compromise and ended up falling in love in the process. Trenton still tore down Kennedi's bakery but chopped off a portion of his casino space. Now Chase Confections would have sizable square footage with dine-in tables and a comfy, leather lounge seating area. The menu would also get an upgrade. Not only would they offer their custom sweet treats but they would expand with gourmet soups, fresh salads, and sand-wiches.

As Tabitha stepped beyond the swing door and crossed the wide hallway, Evie's laughter broke above the rhythmic, soothing sounds of Medasin's "Always Afternoon," one of Tabitha's favorite songs. They often grooved to music in back while they worked.

She entered the side kitchen, the area where custom or-ders were prepared, and froze, going ramrod stiff, her breath catching. There Dominic stood with Evie at the prep table, his attention centered on their current design—a baby cradle. Its blue cake shell sat ready to be covered in pounds of modeling chocolate and sweet vanilla fondant.

The pair's chatter paused as both turned and stared at Tabitha's position by the door. The fact that Dominic always seemed to be dissecting her in an intense, judging scrutiny had her close to walking over and slamming him face-first into that tub of fondant. Despite that, she'd spent a good twenty minutes in the shower placating her sex-starved body with the image of his tall form front and center in her brain. Now he'd shown up at her place of business looking deliciously hot and sexy. Ray-Bans nestled atop a wavy crown of dark hair. A black T-shirt molded the muscular sinews of his upper body. Medium denims encased thick thighs and long legs. Fashionable, black leather lace-up boots with heavy soles covered his feet. His stare in that beautifully chiseled face seemed to draw her from across the room. Another annoyance.

Evie was also to blame. Her talk about Dominic and Tabitha having a connection. And that damn dream she'd had last night of Dominic on his knees in the middle of a torrential downpour, eager to pleasure her in front of a crowd of strangers on the street. *So freaking weird.* And yet, so damn hot. Too hot. Tabitha hadn't really regarded the man in such a light before, which had been well and good with her. But now…

"Tab, there you are. I tried calling you. I was telling Dom that you created the design for the cradle."

Dominic gave a glance over his shoulder at the life-sized structure. "This is amazing. It looks as though an infant could literally sleep in it." His eyes seemed to brighten even more than usual. "It actually has a pillow… Hella cool." He smiled, bringing out that dimple in his cheek.

Evie turned to him. "Isn't it awesome? These gender reveals have gotten elaborate. Tab had the layout configured within hours. She's a master. She's usually the first one here at the crack of dawn, but she had a late evening out." Evie winked. "Hope it went well."

"Really, Evie." Tabitha glared. Of course, the oversharing hardly mattered since Dominic had been a party to her evening. "Thanks for nothing. You were supposed to have my back last night."

"Oh. Right. Sorry. I got tied up here and lost track of time. I'll want the tea later." Smiling, Evie rubbed her hands together, not looking at all contrite. "Every detail."

"Speaking of our date last night…" Dominic said.

"What!" Evie's head swiveled toward him. "You two went out last night? I thought—"

"Evie, don't listen to him." Tabitha shifted her glare to Dominic. "We didn't have a date."

"You made certain we did," he countered, his brow wiggling playfully. "We sat together in a restaurant, ate meals, and shared several bottles of wine. I call that a date."

"Several bottles!" Evie piped in with a grin. Getting a hard, admonishing look from Tabitha, she turned to the baby cradle. "Don't mind me. This modeling chocolate won't shape itself around these spindles."

Tabitha centered on Dominic. "I had only two drinks."

Wearing a crack of a grin, he angled his head to the side, giving him a boyish charm. "I'm pretty sure you had three."

She sighed. "We each had a date."

He rested back against the metal prep table with arms folded across his broad chest. An expanse of delineated muscles displayed a masculine sensuality Tabitha hadn't cared to give much attention before. Recalling how those strong arms felt wrapped around her, she slid her gaze down his frame. Would he measure up to Mr. Big? Her eyes snapped back up. *Stop it!* Was it not enough that she'd pleasured herself to thoughts of him in the shower? She wanted to kick her own ass for once again thinking of him sexually.

"How's ole Randy?" Dominic asked on a chuckle. "The guy didn't look in good spirits when he departed last night."

"I guess Celeste chose to skip breakfast with you," she punched back.

"I dropped her off at her front door following dinner last night, like any respectable gentleman would."

His grin was sinfully wicked, but Tabitha felt a strange sense of satisfaction at hearing that.

"Balaska, why are you here?"

He pulled an iPhone from his back pocket and handed it to her. "It's the latest and greatest. That other one you had—"

"The one you broke."

"The one you dropped," he continued, "likely needed an antenna wrapped in foil to catch a signal."

Evie snickered. "That's funny." She looked at Tabitha and gestured a zip across her lips. "I'm not even here."

"As you can see, it has a shatterproof case and screen protector on the chance you find yourself plotting another date escape attempt."

Tabitha scowled back at his mocking grin. "You're such an..." At Evie's swift reprimanding look, she bit back from calling him an ass of the first order. Instead, she scrolled through the phone's apps, appreciating the big, bright screen, then stuck it in her back pocket. "Thanks."

"You're welcome. It's my understanding you'll be working at Pearl in Vegas for a week during the anniversary. It's definitely a good way to introduce Chase Confections to the West Coast. I'll be in town seeing to things at Shaw corporate and ensuring there are no hiccups with the anniversary schedule. I've informed Etienne Builes, Pearl's executive chef, that you'll be needing space to work in his kitchen. He'll make sure you're situated when you get there."

"Appreciate it."

"I've arranged our departure to leave Reagan National a week from Monday at—"

"I've already booked my flight."

"Cancel it. Trent should've told you we fly private. We'll take Shaw Enterprise's company jet. I added you to the trip's roster. A car will arrive around six a.m. to take you to the airport. I expect you to be on time."

"No, Trent didn't tell me, and like I said, I've already purchased my ticket." She prickled at his highhanded need to control. She didn't like feeling manhandled. Or dictated to, especially by him. "I'll get there when I get there."

His stern gaze held hers, then the tension left his square jaw. "If you get off on flying coach, suit yourself. Your hotel room has been reserved…unless you have a problem with me seeing to that also."

Tabitha didn't push back on that.

"I also stopped by to give you this." He brought up a long, white vinyl tube from the floor, pulled off the plastic cap, and slid out a set of blueprints. "Trent had the plans revised to have the beam shifted three feet to the right like you wanted."

Tabitha lifted an eyebrow. "*Trent* authorized the change, not you?"

"That's right," he answered without even a hint of hesitation. "I don't feel it's worth the thirty-five-thousand-dollar adjustment."

She hadn't realized the cost and felt a hefty helping of

guilt about it but kept a straight face.

Grabbing an apron from the wall hook by the door, she slipped the neck strap over her head and tied it at her back on her way to the sink. While scrubbing her hands, she gave a look at him over her shoulder. "As with the flight arrangements, had you consulted with me before you approved the blueprints, the expense could've been avoided."

"Expect to see the added charge for the redesign on your next invoice."

She shut off the water and swung around. "Invoice? Chase Confections isn't paying for your screwup."

"The beam had been appropriately placed and balanced within the space, but you chose to have it repositioned, so it's at your expense."

Hands dripping wet, she snatched a wad of paper towels, dried off, and flung it into the wastebasket, then crossed to him while considering again, with strong conviction, shoving his head between the spindles of that baby cradle. "Had it been appropriately placed, I wouldn't have moved it." His gaze roamed over her face in a sort of quick study. His scrutiny momentarily landed on her mouth, and he moistened his lips that she knew to be satin soft from when he'd kissed her cheek last night.

Picturing him on his knees with his attractive face buried in her crotch made her swallow a pant. *Shit.*

"Get out of my head—My kitchen! Get out of my damn kitchen."

"Tabitha!" Evie gasped and spun to her. "That's so not cool." She turned to Dominic. "Don't mind her; she apparently woke up on the wrong side of the bed. Can I get you some coffee? How about a freshly baked muffin? Kennedi was here earlier and made her to-die-for blueberry scones."

"I'll pick up a couple on my way out. They're my fav. Good seeing you, Evie. Seils…" Just her name. No Miss. His graceful stride carried him to the door.

"Grab whatever you like. It's always on the house," Evie offered.

"Try the peanut butter-filled ones," Tabitha called out, and his head turned, his expression unamused, then he exited.

"That man!" she gritted out on her stalk to the pantry for the container of blue rolled fondant. "And I'm expected to tolerate him in Vegas for a week. I can't bear being in the same room with him for a minute."

"Why are you so downright mean to Dominic all the time?" Evie's voice was coarse.

Tabitha dropped the container not too lightly on a vacant metal prep table. "He's always trying to control things. I don't like him."

"You mean you don't want to like him, so you strike at him." Evie let go a long sigh. "Real talk, girlfriend. The guy was totally checking you out until you came in here with a heavy dose of attitude and carrying jagged rocks on your back."

"No, he wasn't." Tabitha bristled, hating the sudden internal tug-of-war she'd been undergoing from the moment she left Dominic at the restaurant last night. "This is your fault, you with your psychoanalyzing crap. I was doing just fine before you started in with all this talk about a connection."

"So you admit that you do feel him." Her unyielding gaze was unrepentant. "Sweetie—" the tone of her voice held its familiar comforting caress "—he's not Jeff. You can let yourself like the guy."

"Evie, why aren't you reading this picture? He obviously doesn't like me." Her chest tightened unexpectedly. "I surely don't like him. Now drop it with your textbook diagnosis." She shoved the container across the counter and yanked off the apron, her thoughts jumbled. "Maybe you should've drawn on some of that wisdom when it came to your ex, Patrick. You can't even get him to hand over the key to your BMW. He's got you taking Lyfts and bumming rides. How about you concentrate on fixing your own life for a change?"

Evie flinched, and immediately the cold bitch crown Dominic had bestowed on Tabitha the night before pressed down firmly on her head.

"Hey, I didn't mean—"

"Save it." Evie stalked over to the dock and snatched her phone, cutting the music.

"I'm sorry." Tabitha caught hold of her at the wrist only to have it wrenched away. "Evie?"

The kitchen door opened, and Amy entered. Her eyes darted between them.

"What is it, Amy?" Tabitha asked the young lady who seemed to be holding her breath.

"A customer wants to place a custom cake order. She said she's celebrating her coffee shop's one-year anniversary and is looking for you guys to design something."

"I'll be there in a minute." Amy retreated, and Tabitha turned back to Evie, who'd resumed her work on the cradle.

"I shouldn't have said—"

Evie's head came up from her work. Her green eyes had hardened in a way Tabitha hadn't seen before. She and Kennedi often said their friend held a mild temperament even in the darkest of storms. Evie the arbiter.

"At least I left Patrick and I'm slowly taking back my life. Jeff kicked you to the curb, yet you're still allowing him to control you. He's still renting space in your head for free." She hit back hard, unforgiving, then resumed her task without so much as another glance from her perfectly molded chocolate.

Tabitha winced as the well-deserved rebuke cut marrow deep.

Chapter Five

"HELL YEAH!"

Dominic sprung up from the couch. He delivered a fist bump to Trenton seated in the chair. "That's what I'm talking about."

With a celebratory clink of their beer bottles, they watched the replay as DeMarcus Cousins passed the ball to Steph Curry just above the arc and hit a three-pointer, all net.

The doorbell chimed. With his eyes locked on the seventy-inch wall mount, he walked backward several steps before sprinting barefoot to the foyer and pulling open the door.

"Vin, my man." They gripped palms and pulled into a bro hug before heading into the living room.

Trenton came to his feet and greeted Vincent the same way. "Good game so far."

"I was listening in the car." The two sat in the twin doublewide chairs opposite one another.

Dominic padded across the cool, dark marble tile to his kitchen and grabbed three IPAs. He uncapped them and handed the bottles off as Trenton and Vincent continued laughing it up.

Taking a seat in the center of the couch, he sipped his

beer while he watched the pair who'd been buddies since Scout camp around age twelve. Vincent Scott was now Trenton's personal attorney.

As kids, wherever Trenton went and whatever he did, Dominic tagged behind his big brother. Having taken on the role as Trenton's COO of Shaw Enterprise, one might say that hadn't changed.

Trenton's cell phone rang. He fished it from the front pocket of his jeans. "Dom, it's Mom." Curiosity hung in his gaze. "I wonder what this is about."

With Dominic's father's fatal car accident when he was four and Trenton's biological mother passing away suddenly in her sleep when he was five, they'd bonded easily as brothers from the start when their surviving parents married.

Dominic happily shrugged. It was good not to be on their mom's radar. "She called you, not me." Georgina Balaska Shaw wasn't the sort for light chitchat. Lately, her conversations tended to find a way to remind Dominic of his duties as the heir to the family's yacht business, Balaska Imperial. As if he needed reminding. The company had carried the Balaska name for nearly eighty years. According to his mother, it would reign forever. But the last thing Dominic wanted to do was oversee a ship-building business.

Trenton opened the line. "Hey, Mom. I'm at Dom's with Vincent, watching the game. I'll put you on speaker." He tapped the phone and set it on the center table.

"Perfect. I'll speak to Dominic in a moment. Hello, Vincent."

"Good evening, Mrs. Shaw."

Observing Trenton's cheeky grin, Dom shot him a murderous look. He was not in the mood to listen to their mom scold him about Balaska Imperial. He crossed into the kitchen, but an open floor plan put him at a disadvantage; it didn't prevent him from catching every word.

"Trenton, I've decided to have a little get-together to celebrate your engagement. I'll send the details. The entire family will be attending. Your fiancée's name is Kennedi, correct?"

Trenton sighed. "Mom, you know her name. A get-together isn't necessary."

"Well, apparently it's the only way I'll meet her in person. Skype doesn't allow me to really get to know her."

"Inspect her, you mean," Dominic muttered under his breath on his way back to the couch with a family-sized bag of potato chips.

"You keep saying you'll bring her by but have yet to do so. If I didn't know better, Trenton Alexander, I'd conclude that you don't wish for me to meet her."

Dominic cringed. Using Trent's middle name meant she'd have their asses if they crossed her. Grown-ass men—him pushing thirty-one and Trent nearly thirty-two—yet they wouldn't dare defy her.

"Mom, I do want you to meet her in person. But Kennedi and I have full schedules. She's running a company…make that two companies. And I've had a lot going on with the hotel-casino construction, along with a host of other things."

"Yes, apparently too busy for your mother."

"No, but I'm headed to Dubai and won't be back for at least three weeks. A party really isn't feasible right now."

"Well, then instead I'll prepare a dinner when you return from your trip. Vincent, you're invited as well. I will see you, yes?"

He looked between Trenton and Dominic. Both returned a shrug. "Uh, yes, ma'am."

"Great. Now, Trenton, let me speak to your brother."

On reflex, Dominic caught the cell phone Trenton tossed over like a hot potato as if it scorched his hand. He looked all too happy to get out of the hot seat. "You're on speaker. I can hear you."

"Hello, son. Will I get the pleasure of having both my boys' engagements officially announced at dinner?"

"Mom." Her consistent mission to get him hitched buzzed around him like bees he couldn't swat away. "No, because I'm not engaged to anyone."

"There lies the problem, Dominic Savino. Do you realize what's at stake? Time is running out for you. The trust clause is very clear. You wouldn't want your inheritance forfeited, now would you? You saw what happened to your sister. Balaska Imperial would be in a much stronger position today had Alizka not let the term run out, forfeiting her trust. Such a foolish girl she is. And your cousin, Eaton, is next in line. Maura would love nothing more than to see her son take over Balaska Imperial. It belongs to you. Your father would've wanted to see you run the company, not my cousin's son."

"I'm sure Eaton's handling things. I don't see a problem."

"You wouldn't. All you've ever cared about is that camera of yours." A pregnant pause emphasized her disapproval.

"Your photos are lovely enough, but what use are they?"

"I have a job at Trent's company—you know that."

"I'm aware. Shaw Enterprise wouldn't exist if it hadn't been for your brother. His father practically ran the company into the ground."

"And you refused to help him save it," Dominic grunted.

"Trenton has done well with it on his own. I'm proud of you, my boy." Her voice was raised for Trenton's benefit. "As for you, Dominic Savino, it's understood Eaton is only managing Balaska Imperial until you've settled the trust clause. I'm hoping that will happen soon, son, before he ruins us. His drinking and gambling have gotten out of control. Maura only makes excuses for him. Your father, grandfather, and those before them would roll in their graves if they could witness how Eaton is close to ruining long-standing business relationships. Son, if the company is to survive, you must do what—"

"Okay, okay." Dominic cursed low. "Anything else? I'm missing the game."

"As a matter of fact, yes. I met this lovely young lady today at the salon. Her name's Emily. My usual colorist went home sick. Emily did my color, and it turned out perfect. She's adorable. She's taking evening classes to become a nurse. I told her about you. I'll send you her picture."

"Don't," Dominic gritted out. "Mom, I want to watch the game."

"Fine. Good night. Oh, I expect to see you at dinner as well, understand? Dominic Savino?" she called sharply when he didn't reply.

"Yes. Good night, Mother." He disconnected and met

Trenton's and Vincent's pitying stares.

"Dude." Vincent shook his head and chuckled. "I got flashbacks just now from when we were teenagers."

Dominic got up, scooped the empty beer bottles from the center table, and tossed them into the recycling bin on his way to the bathroom. Short minutes later, he pivoted to the kitchen. "You two up for another?"

Trenton brought up a hand. "Right here."

Vincent gave a look over his shoulder to Dominic in the kitchen. "You've really decided to forfeit your trust fund? You'll be thirty-one in a few months. You have to be married to satisfy it, right?"

"His birthday's December seventh," Trenton supplied. "I highly doubt he'll be happily entrenched in wedded bliss in six months."

"It's a stupid clause," Dominic groused and handed Trenton his beer before dropping back down on the couch. He propped his bare feet upon the center tabletop and snatched the bag of chips from Vincent.

"Trent, you're thirty-one and about to tie the knot. You're not a Balaska by blood, but you've been in the family since you were, what, five?" Vincent asked.

"Six," Dominic corrected.

"Shit, you satisfy the trust as it stands," Vincent said. "Provisional clauses are written all the time. It'd only require all family members to sign off on it."

Trenton sat back. "Our cousin Maura won't sign—of that I can assure you."

"Nope, she won't," Dominic agreed. "It would mean pushing her son, Eaton, even further down the line of succession."

"That's too bad."

"Yes, well, some of us have to build our fortune from the ground up the hard way." Trenton sent a smirk Dominic's way. "Little brother, Mom does have a point. The company is yours to run. Though I'd hate to lose you as my COO."

"If it'd been left up to me, I wouldn't have opted for a damn yacht-building business."

"You're Greek. Ship building is in your Ancestry.com," Vincent lightly teased. "How much of a trust fund are we talking about?"

"About twenty mil, depending on the market," Trenton said, and Dominic nodded. "Another sixty if he produces an heir within the first year."

"Twenty mil." Dominic shot his bother a narrowed side-eye. "That's enough to cover the partnership."

Vincent's eyes went wide. "Dude." He placed his beer on the table in front of him and sat forward, planting his elbows on his knees. "Is that how you're planning to participate in Trent's Dubai partnership? Trent said you want in on the deal. I know the buy-in on the low end to be about fifteen mil."

"Add an extra five for cushion, but yes," Trenton added around a swallow from his bottle.

"Twenty million. Damn." Vincent blew out a breath. "That's no small change to see tossed away. All of the women you've been with and you don't have one prospect on the chessboard?"

"Not one I'd want to chain myself to for life."

"Shit, I'd hire a woman to play the part for that kind of

money," Vincent joked.

"What about your date the other night? Not a contender?" Trenton asked.

Dominic shook his head. "Nah, too clingy."

"How does the trust read exactly?" Vincent questioned, his attorney hat clearly on. "Sometimes there are term-outs."

Dominic shrugged a shoulder. "All I know is I have to be married by age thirty-one to get what's due me." He linked his hands behind his head and cut a look at Vincent. Brown eyes alert, the man's attorney light blinked neon bright, his almond-brown features piqued with interest. "That won't happen in six months, so this conservation is moot. Besides, my mom would expect me to use the funds to grow Balaska Imperial and not invest in Trent's real estate venture." To put an end to the topic, he nodded at the TV. "We're missing the game."

"For a while there, I thought Kennedi's friend and business partner, Tabitha Seils, had slid onto my brother's radar," Trenton said.

"Oh yeah?" Vincent's head moved from Trenton over to Dominic. "What happened?"

"She sticks her nose where it doesn't belong is what happened. We're ten months into construction on that bakery of hers, and just last week she wanted to have a support beam removed."

"That's not completely true," Trenton objected. "In all fairness, she only wanted to have it shifted about three feet to make space for a glass display case."

"And you let her have her way." Dominic cut another harsh look at his brother. "Now she's going to think she can do whatever the hell she wants."

"It's called compromise. I studied the plans. The change didn't really affect the overall layout."

"Yeah, and it only cost you thirty-five grand. She should foot the bill. Whatever," he muttered. "You're about to marry her best friend, so I expect you're buttering up to the Ice Queen of Hearts."

"Ice Queen of Hearts?" Vincent choked a laugh around a swallow of his beer. "That's what you call her?"

"Not to Tabitha's face." Trenton smirked. "He's not that brave."

"She'd just as soon take off my head if given the chance. Though the other night we did manage to get through dinner without—"

"Wait. What?" Trenton shot to the edge of his seat. "Dinner? You and Tabitha had dinner together? She was your date?"

"No. It so happened we both were at Dabney's. Well, she was trying to cut and run out on her date when I came up on her near the bathrooms. The dude was boring as fuck. Stiff as a damn board. I can understand why she wanted to ghost his ass. He's seated next to a beautiful woman and all he can talk about is himself." Trenton and Vincent stared back at him; both wore crooked smirks. "What?"

"You're analyzing the dude and shit." Vincent laughed.

"And you find Tabitha *beautiful*." Trenton continued to grin.

For some strange reason, Dominic simply liked looking at Tabitha. In fact, he couldn't take his eyes off her at dinner. There was something hidden behind that icy exterior that provoked his curiosity. On that, he ignored his brother. "There wasn't much about the dude to figure out. Anyway, Tabitha was trying to do a duck and dodge when I ran into her. Again, can't blame her. The dude didn't strike me as her type."

"Self-absorbed pretty boys with an ego chip on their shoulder aren't her type. I guess that leaves you out," Trenton said on a laugh. "It's what Tabitha said about you the other day."

Dominic scowled. "Ego chip! She said that?"

"Apparently, he's okay with the pretty-boy part," Vincent remarked around a chuckle.

Again, he ignored their laughter at his expense, but something Vincent said earlier sparked an idea. "Vin, you might be onto something with that pretend engagement thing. Tabitha Seils would be the perfect sort for something like that."

Vincent threw a hand up. "Whoa, hold up. I never advised that." He pushed up from the chair and crossed into the kitchen, helping himself to another beer. "In fact, speaking as an attorney, I explicitly advise against it," he called out loudly from across the room.

"What if she agrees to it?" Dominic asked when Vincent returned to his seat.

Trenton laughed. "I can't imagine Tabitha would go along. For starters, she doesn't like you. And second, she really doesn't like you."

Dominic came to the edge of his seat. "Guys, hear me out. As Trent made plainly clear, Tabitha's not into me, not even a little bit. And I'm not into her." A twinge of something he couldn't quite name momentarily knotted low in his gut. "Of course, I'd compensate her for going along. I can get the legal papers inked, thus, satisfying the married bullshit trust clause in order to release the funds and finally get Mom off my back. A win, win, and major win."

Trenton sat forward and shook his head. "Dom, I don't think this is a good idea. In fact, I'm certain it's an insane idea. Kennedi would have my head if she thought I was mixed up in your crazy-ass scheme."

"Maybe something can grow between you two where there won't be a need to pretend. She can't be all that bad, right?" Vincent asked.

"No, she's not," Trenton asserted. "Dom's just not used to a woman calling him on his bullshit."

"What are you talking about?" Dominic bristled. "She's chilly as fuck toward me, has been from the day we met, but I'm the bad guy?"

Trenton grabbed his phone from the couch where Dominic had left it, made a few rapid taps, and tossed the device to Vincent. "That's Tabitha's Facebook profile pic. The rabbits she's holding are named Dixie and Percy."

Vincent shot wide eyes at Dominic. "Dude, are you insane? You're not feeling this sista even a little bit?"

"I never said I didn't find her attractive."

"Oh, she's definitely that." Vincent grinned as he flipped through Tabitha's pictures. "Shit, maybe I should hit her up."

"No!" Dominic rumbled, not sure where the hell that sudden surge of possessiveness sprang up from. He snatched the phone from Vincent. Studying Tabitha's photo—her hair in its usual thick braid, eyes a brilliant wave of sea green woven within rich amber gold, but it was her so rarely seen smile as she cuddled those rabbits that held him captive.

"Judging by the other night, it's a safe bet she's not seeing anyone, so all's good there."

"Of all the stupid things you've done, this would top them all." Trenton sat back and sipped his beer. "It'll be your funeral. On second thought, I'm *telling* you, don't. I can't have you fucking up my relationship with Kennedi by way of some stupid act of yours. Dom, I'm serious. Find someone else."

"I have to agree with Trent. It's an insane idea," Vincent put in. "Besides, she would've probably told your ass to get lost." He laughed.

"Dominic?" Trenton barked.

"Okay, shit, relax. You two have made your point. I'll find someone else."

"Yes, you do that. Stay away from Tabitha Seils. Got it?" Trenton stated firmly.

"I heard you the first time," Dominic ground out.

BALANCING THE FRESHLY baked veggie lasagna at the bend of one arm and cradling a shopping bag with two bottles of Pinot Noir in the other, Tabitha pressed Evie's doorbell with a knuckle. It was their ladies' night in. Movies, munchies, wine, and guy talk. Once a month for the past five years they made time to hang out and hadn't missed one yet.

After a lengthy singsong chime of the doorbell, a second

attempt still resulted in no answer. Yet Kennedi's car sat parked within mere footsteps in the circled driveway of the grand Potomac, Maryland, estate. Given Tabitha's behavior with Evie, her friend's dismissal the past couple of days was severely justified.

She tried the bell again. No answer. Feeling pushed out of the sista circle by her own doing, she pivoted and started down the gray flagstone steps but turned back at the creak of the heavy oak door. Kennedi stood within the frame.

"Hey." Tabitha reversed her steps and gestured at the warm, deep dish she cradled. "It was my turn to cook."

"Evie told me what happened Saturday and that you two aren't speaking."

Tabitha anxiously looked past Kennedi's shoulder for any sign of Evie. "I've tried to talk to her, but she's ignoring me."

"I didn't think you'd come tonight, but I'm glad you're here. To that point—" Kennedi stretched open the door "—you and Evie need to make up, starting with you apologizing for throwing shade on a situation you know she has little control over."

Tabitha stepped into the grand foyer of ivory-colored marble flooring and pristine white, naked walls. Evie had mentioned that Patrick took the expensive art pieces and would return them only if she dropped the separation. *Prick.*

She'd had the nerve to throw salt on her friend's very deep wound while knowing fully Evie had been battling a vindictive and abusive husband. She'd found the strength to leave Patrick, but the man refused to go away quietly.

"I'm guessing Evie doesn't want me here."

"You guessed right, but I stopped that noise. I'm not about to have my two best friends and business partners not speaking to one another." Kennedi took the bag with the wine bottles and led the way into the great room. Twenty-foot vaulted ceilings, retractable skylights, and comfortable, cushy furnishings of warm beiges and soft teal accents sat upon dark hardwood floors.

They crossed into an elegantly dressed kitchen of custom, antique white, raised-panel cabinetry. Evie stood on the opposite side of the enormous, speckled-beige center island, her hands clutching its beveled edge. Her red-wire frames offered no camouflage for eyes that were usually warm but now were filled with discontent.

"Evie, I'm completely at fault." Tabitha didn't hesitate, didn't mince words, fully contrite as she set the warm dish on the counter. "I was wrong to blow up at you. I'm really sorry."

"You should be." Evie huffed and fingered back from her forehead frizzy locks that had escaped her loose ponytail.

"I don't know why Dominic always makes me weird out. I can't explain it."

"I can, but you think my *wisdom* is—"

"I shouldn't have said that." Tabitha rounded the island with arms stretched wide. "Can you forgive me? I made your favorite veggie lasagna, extra spicy with a ton of mushrooms the way you like it." The peace offering entrée didn't erase the grim look shaping Evie's tawny-tan features. "Evie, I was an ass. A major ass. The biggest—"

"Yes, you were." Her lips quirked.

Seeing a small opening of forgiveness, Tabitha wrapped

her arms around her friend. "I'm really sorry." Evie's embrace soon joined in, and they hugged tight. "Love you."

"Love you, too. And I still believe there's something between you and Dom." Evie stepped back. "That's the last I'll say on it."

Tabitha shifted a tentative look between her friends. "I'll admit there's something there, but I can assure you it's one-sided."

"You might be surprised. If you allow a tiny bit of give in the rope, you'll see what I mean. Now I need to make the salad for this lasagna." Her usual easy grin returned as she went to work gathering all of the fixings from the fridge.

"This is an occasion for fine crystal." Kennedi jogged to the wall-mounted control panel and turned on the music, then dance-trotted over to the wine goblets behind the lighted glass-front cabinet. "Ooh, this is my jam."

Tabitha took down plates from the slotted wooden shelf. She could let Evie have the last word on Dominic.

"I'm planning to adopt a baby." She waded through their stark silence for a moment, then turned to see Kennedi and Evie gaping at her.

Holding the stems of three Baccarat glasses pinned between her fingers, Kennedi cut the music. "You're joking, right?"

"Nope, not joking." Tabitha's pulse gave an anxious thump as she heaped generous helpings of the lasagna onto their plates.

"Why?" Kennedi uncorked the Pinot and poured, close to topping the glass.

"Why? Seriously, you would ask me that?" Tabitha

prickled. "You know why. I'm almost thirty, for one thing."

"So are we," Evie said.

"Yes, but you and Kennedi can set your timetable to have a baby whenever you like. I don't have that luxury. I had one shot, and it was wasted on Jeff."

"Don't think like that," Evie said softly. "Tab, you were hit with a lot. Ovarian cancer, the stress Jeff put on you when he backed out of the wedding, losing the baby—"

"His cheating and kicking me out on the street after I'd sold my townhouse—let's not forget that," Tabitha ground out tightly.

Evie nodded. "Jeffrey's a class A dickhead. All of it played a hand in you suffering a miscarriage, but that doesn't mean you can't have another baby. On the contrary, it just means you have to take it easy *when* you become pregnant again."

"The point is, you *can* get pregnant," Kennedi said. "There's no need to adopt for the reason you're giving us. You're also super busy… We all are with the store construction. The craziness will only get worse when we're up and running in the new space."

"You probably should give this more thought," Evie advised. "Look, you know I'm a product of adoption." A stern concern crept into her voice. "I got lucky with parents who are amazing. They fostered me for five years prior to adoption, and put up with me, kept me, even during my horrible adolescent faze. I ran away—twice," she emphasized. "Adoption isn't something you do lightly."

"We don't doubt you'd be a great mother when the time is right. Really consider all of the possibilities, good and bad," Kennedi added.

Tabitha suddenly felt so achingly alone. This was what she'd tried to avoid: the dissuading, the negative commentary. How could she expect them—expect anyone—to understand what she'd lost unless they'd suffered through the crucible themselves? But some small truth carried in their opinion, which she needed to consider. "I'll give it more thought. I should let you know you both may get a call from the adoption agency." Reading their stares of objection, she added, "It's just a formality in case I decide to go through with it."

Chapter Six

"TAB, WHAT ARE you still doing here? You're going to miss your flight."

Tabitha didn't pull her attention away from the one-hundred-and-fifty caffè latte, cup-shaped cakes. "I'm almost done, Kennedi. It took longer than expected for the marshmallow to firm up enough for me to flame." She grabbed the hand torch and carefully toasted the foam-like topping, giving the design a more realistic appearance. "My flight doesn't leave for another four hours. I'm already packed. I just need to shower, grab my bags, and go. I should get to Vegas around ten tonight. Just in time to head straight to bed."

"Yes, but I told you I'd finish these." Kennedi stuck her pinkie in the leftover frosting for a taste. "That's *really* good. You used fine-ground coffee beans in the butter cream, didn't you?"

"Sure did." Tabitha flashed a smile at her before toasting the surface of the last cup. "There. Done." She straightened and pressed her palms to the stiffness in her back. Kennedi brought over a cart and they transferred the trays of desserts. "Mrs. Taylor will be in around ten tomorrow morning to pick these up." Tabitha rolled her finished work into the walk-in fridge, then moved back to the table and began cleaning up. "The Masons should arrive about the same time for the cradle."

Kennedi snatched the kitchen towel from her hand. "I got this. Go catch your flight."

Tabitha looked around the kitchen—every pot, pan, and utensil in perfect order. She wasn't looking forward to working in a space that wasn't considered her domain.

"Don't forget about Dixie and Percy."

"Evie and I will take care of your rabbits. Don't worry. You should try to see a show while you're in Vegas. I hear the Zumanity Cirque du Soleil is a must-see performance." A comforting arm draped Tabitha's shoulders. "And I need you to do me a major favor."

"What is it?"

"Please try to get along with Dom. He's Trent's brother and you're my best friend. Maybe you could use this time to try to get to know him a bit better. He's actually a nice guy."

"If you say so." Tabitha had yet to see it.

"At least say you'll try. Like Evie said, allow a little slack in the rope." Her soft smile of encouragement made it worth giving in to the idea.

"Fine, I'll try." Saying the words was easy to do. Executing them?

"WHAT DO YOU mean, you don't have my reservation?" It was the last thing Tabitha wanted to hear after having sat next to two teenagers cackling while saying *and like* between every other word, decimating the English language, for nearly six hours. Talk about karma being a bitch. It was grand payback for turning down the private flight accommodations Dominic had offered.

She glanced behind her at the parade of bodies crowding Shaw Hotel and Casino's grand lobby. The place was crazy busy for eleven o'clock on a Monday night.

Exhausted, she took a long breath to draw on a sliver of patience and smiled at the desk attendant, who was shuffling papers and dropping pens. Doug, according to the name badge on his royal-blue blazer, appeared a bit stressed himself. "I flew in from D.C. and have been up since five a.m., East Coast time. I have an early start tomorrow, so I really need my room."

"Maybe I'm not keying it in correctly. Sorry, I just started this morning." He gave her an apologetic look and asked for assistance from his colleague, Bethany, as her name badge indicated. The young woman handed room keycards to the couple she'd been helping and offered them a polite good night. Then she brushed her red ponytail back over her shoulder and made a few taps on Doug's keyboard. "Let's see if we can find you."

As the two combed through the reservations, Tabitha pointed to her ID that Doug held. "It's Seils with an I instead of an A." The young woman's crinkled brow beneath her sparse bangs said the results of her search would conclude the same. "It's not there. Terrific," Tabitha bit out.

"When did you make the reservation?" Doug asked.

"Doug, look, that's her."

Tabitha turned her head in the direction of Bethany's

outstretched index finger. *What the...!* She caught sight of a not-so-appealing picture of herself on one of the huge flat screens affixed to the enormous marble pillar that centered the fountain. Beside that awful photo for Pearl Fine Dining restaurant was the caption: *D.C.'s Chase Confections's master pastry chef, Tabitha Seils, celebrates Shaw's 5th anniversary by showcasing her delicious custom dessert creations, sure to tantalize the palate.*

Small ad, my ass. It was playing on a loop among a host of other promos. Kennedi and Evie were cropped out of the photo. It had to be Balaska's doing. *A heads-up would've been nice.*

Jaw clenched, she turned back to the pair who stared at her, wearing wide smiles. "This is a lesson for me to handle my own accommodations in the future. Mr. Balaska must have—"

"Did you say Balaska?"

"Yes, he made the reservations."

Bethany's mossy-green eyes widened. "Oh." Her fingers flew across the keyboard. "We apologize, Miss Seils, for the confusion. Doug will get you settled in." She directed the young man's attention to something on the computer screen before stepping back to her station.

"Miss Seils, sorry for the inconvenience. Here's your keycard. The private elevators are on the right. The gentleman there will assist you."

Tabitha swiveled around. As if out of nowhere, a valet attendant stood at attention behind her. Somehow Doug had sent out some sort of silent beckoning.

"I can manage," she told the valet.

"It's no trouble."

"Enjoy your night, Miss Seils." Doug smiled warmly.

She followed the valet, who insisted on seeing her and her luggage to penthouse suite number one, according to the plaque on the wall. "I can manage from here." She handed him a twenty-dollar bill. It was Vegas. And the penthouse. Anything less seemed like an insult in a five-star luxury hotel.

"If there's anything I can do for you, please don't hesitate to call. Have a good night."

"Good night." She swiped her keycard at the stark white double doors, entered, and clicked the wall switch just inside. "Holy shit!" The place was enormous and beyond absolutely beautiful. She smiled. *Okay, Balaska, you get a check mark for this one.*

The foyer led two steps down into a spacious living area of white deep-cushioned furnishings. The place had a full kitchen with breakfast bar on her left. Across the room, glass French doors that opened to a wide balcony were set within a wall of naked windows that offered a beautiful nightlife cityscape of the Strip. Two sets of bedroom double doors stretched open wide at the left and right of the living space. Far too exhausted to give herself the full tour, she crossed back to the entryway to turn off the light, reversed steps, and pivoted right simply because that bedroom was the closest.

The table lamp offered the low light needed to grab her toiletry bag along with a white lace tank and matching boy shorts. She went into the adjoining bathroom. A motion sensor flickered, illuminating the room. "My goodness!" A huge, rectangular, jetted tub centered the space of more glossy white marble floors that traveled midway up the walls.

A flat screen separated twin sinks that were decked out in high-polished chrome fixtures. A gas fireplace within a wall niche added to the luxurious décor. The shower that practically took up an entire wall had clearly been designed for two. Maybe three.

She started the rain nozzle before quickly stripping out of her clothes, undoing her braid, and stepping beneath the warm spray. The water beating against her tired limbs soothed. Eyes closed, she was tempted to fall asleep right where she stood.

Finally, seated on the edge of the bed, she plaited her thick mane—tangles be damned come morning—and secured it beneath a pink satin wrap.

Her cell phone chimed in her handbag. The expected group text from Kennedi and Evie; they checked in on one another every night. Tabitha sent them the all-good thumbs-up emoji, too tired to say more.

As with the living room, there were no coverings of any kind to block the city lights that poured in through the huge wall of glass and French doors. How could anyone sleep like this? Thankfully, she'd brought along her sleep mask and made a mental note to contact the concierge in the morning.

The premium thread count felt heavenly against her skin as she slipped beneath the cozy bedding and turned off the lamp. Sleep easily claimed her almost the moment her mask came down over her closed lids.

DOMINIC CROSSED THE lobby to the elevator. He'd waded

through a full day of appointments from the moment he stepped off the plane. His evening had been swallowed up by back-to-back meet-and-greet events. Exhausted and fighting a migraine that had been pounding in the center of his skull all damn day, he looked forward to his bed.

It was closing in on midnight, yet the lobby was bustling with activity. Nice to see business was good. The anniversary promos had been successful, so much so that Shaw had met its projected annual revenue in only the second quarter.

As the elevator carried him up, he considered texting Tabitha to see if she'd made it in okay but thought better of it. The last thing he needed was a fight with her. Everything between them tended to be a battle, at least when it came to him. Tabitha Seils flat-out abhorred him. He hadn't a clue why.

At the door of his suite, he swiped his keycard while yanking loose his tie. It was his private residence when in town. He didn't bother turning on any lights, allowing the illumination of the city filtering through the bare windows to guide his steps.

He sat on the couch, appreciating the comfort, and took off his shoes, then shrugged out of his suit jacket. The deep plush cushions called to him. Forcing himself up, he trudged into the bedroom, stripped down to bare skin, and crawled between the covers, hoping sleep would offer much-needed relief for his pounding cranium. Come morning, he'd have to face Tabitha, who would surely bring about more of the same.

Tabitha roused awake from the sound of a thump. She slid the eye mask up her forehead and listened. Quiet. Well-insulated walls kept noise to a subtle thud now and then.

She squinted at the glare of the city lights beaming in through the windows, then glanced at the digital clock on the nightstand—1:52 a.m. In need of a glass of water, she rolled out of bed and padded to the kitchen. The sight of muscular calves and large bare feet—the only parts of the intruder that were visible from within the open door of the fridge—drew her up short. Without thinking, she charged, spun with a roundhouse kick, a move she'd learned in her muay Thai self-defense class, and landed a heel center mass into the door. The move knocked the individual clear off his feet, dropping him where he stood.

"Don't move! I've already called security." A scare tactic to gain seconds as she frantically ran her hands over the wall and found a switch. The room lit bright. In full defense mode, she glanced around for a weapon of any kind.

"What the hell, woman!"

Tabitha spun. "Dominic?" She looked down at the figure sprawled out on the floor...completely naked. *My goodness!* Her gaze flew to the ceiling and back to him in stunned disbelief, then again skyward, back and forth, unable to stop. "What the hell are you doing in my room? And without any clothes on?"

He groaned. "I think you gave me a concussion on top of my splitting skull." Palming the top of his head, he trudged with some effort to his feet. "What the hell do you mean, your room? This is my suite."

She took in a quiet breath at the sight of his stunningly

carved physique. "Your suite?"

"Precisely." He opened the freezer and retrieved an ice cube that he pressed smack against his brow while almost stumbling over to stand behind the metal barstool.

The tall chair shielded very little. A dusting of dark hair split his swollen pecs. Bulging arms and shoulders. Six-pack abs. Thick thighs. And all beneath the glow of well-tanned skin. Goodness, he was a living sculpted masterpiece.

The man's cock was huge… Tabitha did her best to keep her eyes fixed chest high but was failing miserably. "Why are you naked? Damn it, put some clothes on, why don't you?"

His gaze slid down her body, and, realizing her own state of undress, she hurried back to the bedroom and slipped on a T-shirt and yoga shorts. When she returned, she found him seated on the couch in a plain white T-shirt and black jersey knit shorts. His eyes were closed with his head tilted back against the sofa spine; his palm still lay pressed to his head. She sat on the opposite couch across the oval glass table, facing him. "You said you booked my room. They couldn't find my reservation but then gave me this room."

"I did book it, and I can assure you it wasn't in here. This is my private suite. It's where I stay when I'm in town. The clothes hanging in the closet and personal effects should've been your first clue." His voice was gravelly low, as if it hurt to speak.

She looked around at the beautiful photography artwork of landscapes and seascapes mounted behind frameless glass and nicely furnished décor that appeared cozier than the standard hotel norm. "I didn't go into the other bedroom. Obviously, the attendant made a mistake in assigning me this suite."

"Obviously," he muttered.

Watching him suffer, she felt bad for ramming him with the refrigerator door. "Sorry about earlier. I thought you were an intruder." He cracked open an eye and squinted at her, staring…or glaring. She couldn't quite tell. "What? It was dark. How was I to know it was you?"

The space between his blue eyes pinched before his lids shuttered again.

"Your head hurts that bad?"

A grunt was his only reply.

Feeling partially responsible for his discomfort, she went into the bedroom and grabbed a small tincture from her bag, then returned to him and peeled his hand away from his head. "Here, let me—"

"Whoa." He drew back, grabbing her wrist, stalling her hand that held the bottle over his forehead. "What's that?"

"Peppermint oil. It'll help relieve the pain. Lavender oil would work better, but this is all I have with me." He didn't look convinced; his features tightened. "Relax, it's not going to kill you. See?" She sprinkled a few drops on the back of her hand and rubbed it in. "Evie makes it. I sometimes get a headache when I fly. I used to be a skeptic, too, but she knows her stuff."

Adding drops on the tips of her fingers, she stepped between the split of his long legs, and he seemed to press himself away deep into the sofa cushion. *Ookay.*

Ignoring the mental slap, she lightly stroked across his brow and along his temples, circling slowly with her thumbs. She eased her fingers into his hair. Dark, silky strands brushed feather-soft against her skin as she gently massaged his scalp. He stared at her, unblinking in that dissecting sort of way, like someone studying a puzzle they couldn't figure out.

"Do you get headaches often?"

"It usually happens when I don't eat."

"Why didn't you eat? That's not healthy."

"Busy day. No time."

"Make time." She purposely made her tone brusque while continuing the rotating motion at his temples, working the area for long minutes, then stepped back. His wary gaze softened, though his stare never left her face the entire time. "How's that?"

"It still aches."

"You have to give it time." She started her ministrations again while marveling at his handsome features. The tension left his shoulders, and he closed his eyes on a long sigh.

Did he have kids? What sort of dad would he be? Likely the stern, eat your vegetables sort. But that would be a good thing because she'd be easily swayed by their little cherub's face—

What am I saying?

She jerked her hands away, and his eyes fluttered open. "You might also be a bit dehydrated," she said on her way into the kitchen, needing a moment of space. *Where in the hell did that thought come from?* In no universe would Dominic and she have a baby, even by way of adoption. She almost laughed out loud at the ludicrous thought.

She filled a glass with water and brought it to him. He watched her over the rim as he swallowed down large gulps.

His study of her provoked a sense of inadequacy, a cube wedged in a round hole. Evie had misread the tea leaves. Nothing about the way he eyed Tabitha said *I'm interested in you*.

"Thanks."

"You're welcome." She set her shoulders back on a quiet exhalation, uncoiling the sudden knot of tension rolling through her and letting her pride muscle through. "I'll see about getting my room in the morning, one with drapes. How can you get any sleep in this place without any window treatments? I can only imagine what it's like when the sun comes up."

He retrieved the remote from the side table and aimed it at the wall of windows while pushing to his feet. A blackout shade slid down between the apparent double panes of glass.

"Until then, good night, Miss Seils." His tone about as empty as the glass she now clutched in her hand, he strode into the bedroom and closed the door behind him.

But not before she caught a silhouette of that nicely sculpted ass bathed in the city lights as he peeled out of those shorts.

Chapter Seven

DOMINIC SLID IN between the cool sheets and crawled over her. He licked the warm pulse along the arch of her neck and pushed the delicate lace of her top aside to feel her soft breasts, each so perfectly proportioned to her slender frame. He captured a pebbling nipple between his lips, his ravenous mouth taking long pulls, his tongue circling the rosy areolas, from one to the other, and flicking the stiff peaks.

"Dominic," she breathed. Her fingers threaded through his hair, fisting the thick mane, holding him in place as he took his fill.

He explored her lean body, charting perfect curves and soft angles, slipped his hand inside her panties and found her clit, teasing the tight bud before burrowing a digit deep within her clenching, wet pussy. As his gaze held hers, her hips rocked in a synchronized rhythm with his measured strokes. "Tabby, it's been you, only you."

Her eyes closed on a long, breathy wail that grew louder and louder until—

Dominic was jolted awake by his ringing cell phone. The air heavy in his lungs, he felt nearly out of breath. And he was swollen hard as a fucking stone. *Shit, not again.* What was he, fucking fifteen again? Slowly, he rolled to his back, thankfully free of head pain. Usually he'd wake after a migraine to a dull throbbing. But not this morning, at least not in his skull. The oil seemed to have done the trick.

Aside from not eating, nothing else about his routine had changed to provoke the sudden spike in headaches lately. Except for the rough sleep and incessant erotic dreams he'd been having for nearly a week that centered on Tabitha. After seeing her in that white lace tank and panties last night, he could now confirm her body was as perfect as his nighttime fantasy had conjured up.

He grabbed the cell phone from the nightstand and opened the line to his brother while checking the time—ten after seven. "Yeah," he breathed out, releasing the pressure in his chest.

"Tell me you're not still in bed?"

"You do realize I'm three hours behind you."

"Get up. I need you to make certain Tabitha is settled in at Pearl. As you said, Etienne can be difficult. I received an email from him just yesterday complaining about how she'll disrupt his kitchen, its orderliness."

Dominic pinched the sleep out of his eyes. "Yeah, he's made his objection very clear to me, too. Said she'll get in his way."

"Which is why you need to keep the peace. Both of them are used to being in charge."

Judging how Tabitha had sent Dominic flat on his ass last night—no need to share that with his brother—heads were sure to butt between her and Etienne.

Dominic got up, cracked open the door, and gave a peek.

The other bedroom's double doors were open. The place was quiet. *She's already gone.*

He padded to his bathroom en suite. "I got it covered. I have a few promo interviews for her lined up, and other events this week as well. It'll give Etienne some space."

"Good. Let me know how it goes. And, bro, I know you and Tabitha don't see eye to eye on much."

"On anything," Dominic mumbled around his sonic toothbrush.

"I suggest you use this time to try to work out your differences with her. Tabitha and Kennedi are practically sisters. I'd really like to see you two get along. Hey, this might help—I discovered from Kennedi that Tabitha's big into working out. You have that in common," he said with a lift in his voice, like it was some big, encouraging tidbit.

Dominic spit out the toothpaste and rinsed. "The ice queen is into health and fitness. Lucky me."

A heavy sigh flooded the line. "Dude, calling her names isn't how you start a peacekeeping mission. I need you to make an effort."

"I've tried to make an effort for damn near a year."

"Yeah, by labeling her an ice queen. Try damn harder." Sternness replaced encouragement. "I leave for Dubai this afternoon. I don't need to be concerned about this. I need you to make this work."

"I'll check in later." Dominic hung up and felt an immediate twinge of guilt. Calling Tabitha ice queen had indeed been unfair, at least if he were to go off her behavior last night. She'd tended to his headache with a surprisingly warm and gentle nurturing when she could've let him suffer.

She smelled good last night, like fresh berries. Her scent, a soothing intoxication, had helped ease the pounding in his head. He found her so mesmerizingly beautiful yet so frustrating in the same breath.

If his dreams were any indication, there was no question he was absurdly attracted to her. And if he were truthful with himself, her bossy attitude was kind of a turn-on. Even the way she wore her hair in that no-nonsense, *I have shit to do* single braid gave him a rise. He chuckled inwardly at the ridiculousness. *I must be out of my damn mind.*

His phone rang again as he had one foot into the shower. He checked the display—the concierge.

"Morning, Wes."

"Good morning, Mr. Balaska. I hate to disturb you at such an early hour, but I wanted to let you know I've been made aware of the mishap with Miss Seils's reservation. I can assure you, sir—"

"Just Dominic or Dom will do." The guy had only recently come on board and was hardly much older than Dominic himself. "I'm about to shower. I'll come find you in an hour. We can discuss it then."

"Yes, of course."

Dominic made quick work of shampooing his hair. But even soap in his eyes couldn't erase the vision of Tabitha in that white, lace top that offered little camouflage of her rosy dark nipples. *That body. Legs for days. And a tattoo. Go figure.* The black outline of a leafy branch rode the well-defined curve of her right pelvis, snaking downward, disappearing within those matching lace panties. His tongue would trace the intricate pattern…

Shit. Having a vivid image of the woman's body swimming around in his head wouldn't help rid him of those damn dreams by any stretch. And his enjoyment of her faintest touch… *Enough!* He shook Tabitha out of his head. He had about as much of a chance with her as he would taming a snake. She'd made it vividly clear he wasn't her type. Getting her out of his suite and settled into her own room was priority one. Dominic drew on that as he focused on the matters of the day. Another full schedule ahead of him, and it would likely begin with sending Tabitha and Etienne to their opposite corners. No doubt she'd want complete reign over the man's kitchen.

Fan-fucking-tastic.

Chapter Eight

THE STAFF AT Pearl had table dressings underway. The restaurant didn't normally open until five thirty in the evening, but seating would start at noontime throughout the anniversary month.

Pearl had done well in the three years since its opening day. Introducing D.C.'s renowned Chase Confections and its custom creations, as it'd been promoed, to the dessert fare meant the high-dollar restaurant's milieu had essentially become the must go-to in Vegas. Like the hotel, the place was booked solid.

He crossed the dining room to the kitchen. No pots and pans were being hurled about. Dominic considered that a good sign. The air, already thickly scented with varying delectable flavors, carried him onward. Everyone moved about like a synchronized, well-oiled machine. Etienne Builes's boisterous laughter rose above the chatter and clink of dishes and utensils. That was new. Dominic had hardly ever seen the Frenchman's strong, ebony features crack a grin… Maybe once or twice when he'd sampled a taste of his own perfect creation.

The executive chef came from the back, suited in his customary crisp, white jacket and black slacks. Tabitha was at his side. Instead of her signature pale pink T-shirt with its white scripted *Chase Confections* logo across the breast and her hip-hugging denims, she wore a pale pink chef jacket and perfectly fitted black slacks. Her long braid lay draped over her right shoulder. Her cheeks carried a natural blush. Both chefs were laughing heartily. A peculiar tightness came into Dominic's chest. Her ebullient look, one that extended to her brilliant hazel eyes, was about the prettiest he'd ever seen. He watched as the amusement in her cheerful gaze dimmed like a burner cooling at seeing him across the long, metal prep station.

Why does she despise me so?

He approached the pair and met Etienne's six-foot-two, broad frame at eye level. The man resembled more of a boxer than an unrivaled French culinary genius. "I see you two have become acquainted."

"That we have." Etienne delivered a grin to Tabitha beside him. "She has already blended in well with the team."

"You've made it easy." Tabitha waved a hand at the large workstation behind them that held an array of pastry items. "I have more than enough space to work." She turned to Dominic. "Etienne has made sure I have everything I need. One of his junior chefs, Andreas there, will be assisting me." She pointed at a young man who was putting pans away. "I've created some of the items I'm considering for the dessert menu."

Dominic gave a look over her shoulder at the powdered sugar-winged doves perched in a pool of raspberry puree-like base, star-shaped pies, a variety of miniature cakes, and, of course, Shaw's logo, the Triton, shaped out in a firm chocolate fudge cake and centered in what appeared to be a heavy whipped cream concoction. *Well, damn.* It was closing in on nine a.m. He could only imagine what she'd accomplish in a full day.

"I see you've been busy this morning."

"Her hands were deep in dough when I got in around six." Etienne stepped over to the table. "I've sampled just about everything." He looked back at Tabitha with a sure-fire smile. "Delicious. The blueberry pie with goat cheese is about the best I've tasted."

"Thank you." She returned the gesture in kind.

Dominic could read Etienne's expression from a mile away. Clear admiration and respect filled the man's gaze.

Tabitha's cell phone rang. "Excuse me." She retrieved it from her pocket and stepped away.

Dominic moved to Etienne's side. "Glad to see you two sharing space won't be a problem. I know you had some reservations about having her here."

"It was before I knew what a delight she'd be. Did you know she likes rock climbing? I'm talking actual scaling, not that indoor stuff. And she's into UFC." He gaped with a grin. "I don't know about you, but I find that appealing."

That last little get-to-know-you came as no surprise after her performance when Dominic found himself ass-flat on the floor.

He tried to keep his features from betraying his growing irritation. Ten months…hell, he'd known Tabitha for damn near a year. Etienne had hardly met her a minute ago and likely knew her most secret of secrets. The notion dug underneath Dominic's skin, but it was the marrow-deep offense that surprised him the most. "Miss Seils won't have much time for any of that while she's here."

"I won't have time for any of what?" Tabitha returned to them.

"I told Dominic that you and I shared earlier some of the things we like to do," Etienne said. "Terrific chefs aside—" his grin was still in place "—it turns out we have a lot in common."

Tabitha pivoted her head to Dominic. "We thought it'd be a good way to break the ice," she rushed out with her eyes on his, her tone almost confessional.

Dominic gave a nod while struggling to remain aloof. "Etienne, can you give us a minute?"

"Of course. It's chaotic in here. Feel free to use my office if you like."

"Thanks." He had to broaden his steps to catch up with Tabitha, who'd already marched off toward the back of the kitchen and down a short hallway.

He followed her into the small, windowless room and closed the door. They stood facing one another for a quiet moment. Her eyes winged upward slightly at the outer corners. Her rosy lips had a natural pucker. *Focus on the matter at hand.*

"About your hotel accommodations—"

"How's your head? Feeling better?"

He blinked, thrown off for a moment. He could still feel her slender fingers in his hair, gently stroking away the gnawing ache. "Yes. Thanks."

"Good. As for my room, I spoke with the concierge. I believe Weston is his name. The rooms are entirely booked.

I'll be staying at The Venetian. Etienne said he can pick me up in the morning. It's on his way. I won't need a car service."

"No, you'll stay with me," Dominic blurted and blinked again, not sure what possessed those words to fall from his lips, yet he didn't want to pull them back.

"No need. My luggage has already been sent to the hotel."

"I'll arrange for the return. There's enough space for both of us in my suite."

"I don't—"

"Look, you have a tight itinerary. And given you like to start your day at the crack of dawn, it would put you at an inconvenience to not stay on the premises. Not to mention, my brother would have a coronary if he discovered you had to stay off-site."

"Are you sure? I don't want to get in your way, prevent your leisurely late-night stroll in your birthday suit." Her lips curved a slight grin.

"If I wasn't sure, I wouldn't have suggested it." Her brow lifted, and he realized his tone was unnecessarily combative.

His phone chimed in his pocket. He checked the display—a meeting notification reminder.

"On the agenda today, I've scheduled you a sit-down at one o'clock with Miranda Edwards. She's with KLAS, the local news station. Tomorrow you'll talk with Ben Dunlevy. Same time. He has a column in the *Vegas Sun*. Both will meet you here. They'll want to sample your desserts. Judging by what I saw, I think you have that part covered."

"What am I expected to say to them?"

"They'll ask the questions. Just keep your responses brief. Don't overshare. You seem to manage that well enough with some. I guess we can't all be Etienne." That small dig spilled out like a formidable grenade. *Shit.*

"What is that supposed to mean?" Her head tilted to the side, her expression returning to all hard angles.

"I'm late for a meeting over at corporate." Not wishing to delve into his seesaw mood, he checked his watch and pulled opened the door as an odd jumble of irrational emotions stirred.

"Will you be here for the interview?" she asked on their way back into the kitchen. She stopped at her station and grabbed oven mitts, slipping them on while moving to the stove.

"Yes, I'll be plugging Shaw's anniversary, of course. Call if you need anything." He continued but turned around when she called his name. "Yes?" The familiar aroma of sweet blueberries reached his nose the moment she cracked open the oven.

"I made you scones. I kept them warm in case you stopped by. Didn't want you to miss breakfast again." She individually wrapped three of the warm, flaky pastries and placed them carefully in a box. "I remembered you once said they were your favorite. Anyway, here you go."

In that moment, every ounce of pent-up aggression toward her dissipated. The idea that she would consider his needs nearly knocked him back on his heels. And the fact that she could control his emotions that easily was also kind of scary.

Her defined right eyebrow rose, and Dominic came out

of his stare as he glanced at the box in her outstretched hand. "Appreciate it." He kept his voice dispassionate mainly so as not to delve more into why she would've done something so considerate, an act out of character where he was concerned. *Last night and now this. What's happening?*

"See you later then?" she asked.

He nodded, and she went about her work. As he headed out, he told himself not to look back but felt a nagging pull to do it anyway. He gave a look over his shoulder and released a quiet breath to relieve the familiar clench in his chest. Her eyes were already locked on him from across the room. A hint of a smile creased her lips before she looked away.

Well, damn.

Chapter Nine

ALASKA, WHERE ARE you?

Tabitha trekked a tight pace in Etienne's office. The reporter was due to arrive any minute. What should she say that would be of any real fascination? Kennedi handled the marketing and business relations for Chase Confections. Interviews were more her expertise. Even Evie would've been far better at taking an interview.

Her cell phone's ring gave her a start. She rushed to answer it—hopefully, it was Dominic to say he was on his way—but it was Kennedi. *Perfect timing.* "Kenni, so glad you called. I need your help."

"What's wrong?"

"I have an interview with a local news reporter any minute. I'm starting to freak out a little. This is your wheelhouse. You should've been the one to come to Vegas, not me. Why you and Evie felt I'd be—"

"Okay, breathe." Kennedi let out a slow breath, and Tabitha followed suit. "I couldn't go. I need to stay close to home to keep an eye on my father. His health is stable right now, but given his dementia, it's important that I not travel too far. And Evie's picking up the slack at the boutique."

Tabitha had no qualms about any of that. She was just a

bit on edge. "I understand. I don't want to screw this up."

"You won't. Typically, the reporter will ask direct questions about the bakery and about the sort of items we make. I find it best to keep it short."

"That's what Dominic said. He also said he'd be here to talk about Shaw's anniversary, but of course, he's late. I should've known he'd leave me hanging, just as he did with my hotel reservation." She started pacing again. A habit she'd picked up from Kennedi, no doubt. Her friend could wear a crater in the tile when she became stressed.

"How did he screw up your reservation?"

"The hotel didn't have my room. Long story, but I spent the night in his suite, and I'll be staying with him for the duration."

"His suite…sharing a bed?"

"No! Of course not." Tabitha rolled her eyes on a sigh. "Don't get it twisted. He has a private residence at Shaw's. It's a two-bedroom suite. The place is huge." She sat on the corner edge of the desk to prevent driving a groove into the floor. "Kenni, uh, about Dominic. I made him scones this morning."

"Really! That's great."

"Great, huh?" Tabitha scoffed. "His vibe said he wasn't feeling it. He probably dumped them in the trash."

"Tab, come on. I'm sure he saw the gesture for what it was."

"You didn't see his face. I tried to take your and Evie's advice, but the man simply doesn't like me. Trust me, there's nothing there, at least on his end. It was stupid of me to even try."

"It's good that you're making an effort. Keep it up. You two are a lot alike. You both like to take the lead."

"That may be, but I know when a guy is into me, and Dominic clearly isn't. Anyway, that's not important right now. He should be here."

"Have you tried calling him?"

"He's not answering."

"I'm sure he has good reason. I can have Trent call him."

"No, I'll go it alone." It was pretty much the familiar safe lane she rode in anyway. "I'll manage." She came to her feet. "He can—"

"Miss Seils, there you are."

Tabitha whirled around to find Dominic in the doorway. Contrary to her decree made mere seconds ago, an undeniably large dose of relief washed over her. "I have to go."

"Did I hear Dom?" Kennedi asked.

"Yes. I'll call you later." Tabitha paused. "You called me. Did you need something?"

"Evie and I received a call from the Parker Adoption Agency. Also, I may have found the perfect bridesmaid dress. I think you'll like it. I'll send you a picture. We can discuss both when you're free. Take care."

They disconnected. *Parker Adoption.* Tabitha's stomach flipped on its side. The interviews with her friends and family had apparently started. As for the dress, Kennedi had been given only one request: no ruffles. Tabitha pushed both matters aside and moved to Dominic. "You're late, and you didn't answer your phone."

He glanced at his watch. "I have five minutes, which says I'm early." He cut a grin, amplifying his easy good looks, and pulled his phone from his pants pocket. "I'd put it on mute while in a meeting. I guess I forgot to take it off."

"You think?"

"Hey, Tabitha, the reporter's here."

They pivoted their heads to Andreas standing in the hall. "We're on our way." Tabitha turned back to Dominic and looked up into those astoundingly blue irises touched by ice crystals. What puzzled and fascinated her were the fine twin grooves that appeared and disappeared between those orbs. What was going on in that head of his when he looked at her in this all-encompassing way? "I didn't think you were coming." Why had her voice suddenly dropped to a husky timbre?

"I said I'd be here. I'm a man of my word." His tone matched hers, his cool gaze unwavering.

Both stood quiet, merely studying the other.

"I guess we should get going." Tabitha gestured a hand at the empty hallway.

"Right."

Neither moved for a silent moment.

She stepped out, but he caught her wrist in a light hold and slowly drew her in, so close she could feel his heat.

"Your hair. Here." He tucked loose unruly coils that had escaped her braid back behind her ear. With his eyes never leaving hers, the tips of his fingers gently glided slowly downward, grazing the side of her neck, lingering. "There. Back to perfect."

"That was a close one." She attempted a light playfulness. He smiled, but then blinked, and what she thought had been a hint of something in his gaze reverted back to his usual aloof countenance just as quickly. Yet it didn't stop her skin from growing warm or her pulse from stirring.

"We should go." He stepped out, moving with an all-business stride.

They entered the kitchen. A cameraman had set up his tripod at Tabitha's workstation. Another man was erecting white umbrella screens with strategic efficiency for optimal lighting on the table of desserts. Across the kitchen, Miranda Edwards ended her chat with Etienne. Her nude, stiletto heels tapped the tile as she came forward.

"Miss Seils, it's a pleasure to meet you. When Dominic called me asking to do a segment on Chase Confections coming to Pearl, it was an easy yes. My sweet tooth can sometimes rule me." She gave a playfully familiar touch on Dominic's forearm. "He knows me well. Dominic swears by your desserts, couldn't stop raving about all Chase offers. I can't wait to dig in."

Tabitha noted the feral smile that slashed Dominic's lips, and read between the lines. Tall, leggy, beautiful, life-size Barbie—of course she would be his type. Disappointment etched a sharp fracture in her mood. The feeling was illogical. Ridiculous, even. Dominic and Tabitha would hardly be labeled as friends. More like necessary acquaintances. Yet she couldn't shake the loss. Valerie, Celeste, and now Miranda—women who easily bent to his charm, a magnetism he stingily withheld from her.

"We're ready." The cameraman aimed his lens. The spotlights flickered on, nearly blinding her in the already brightly lit kitchen.

"I'm here with Tabitha Seils of Chase Confections, one

of D.C.'s finest bakeries. So, Tabitha, tell me a little about your store."

Tabitha recast her expression into one of authority and met Miranda's inquisitive blue eyes with a small smile. "I'm one of three partners, Evie Powell and Kennedi Chase. Kennedi's mother opened the store over thirty years ago. Some of our desserts are her mother's recipes, with a twist here and there. My partners and I have added our own ideas."

"I read that you, in particular, use words like, 'a pinch,' 'a hint,' 'a dash,' which makes it difficult for anyone to pin down the ingredients. No one can get it just right, but you."

Tabitha raised a brow, impressed and returned her smile. "You do your homework, Ms. Edwards."

"That I do."

"Well, what I've prepared today is a small sample of the delectable creations we offer." Tabitha answered a few more questions, and Dominic added his input.

"What do you suggest I try first?" Miranda eyed the table.

"I say try the blueberry pie. You won't regret it," Dominic suggested.

"Dominic, you would." Another playful nudge. "But I think I actually will have a taste of the pie."

Tabitha pulled her gaze away from the pair and plated a slice. She handed it to Miranda, who forked a small bite. The woman's eyes closed, and she moaned as she took a second taste.

"It's really delicious. The blueberries burst on your tongue." Next, she tried the bourbon-infused chocolate

Triton cake. "Oh my God! This is sinful."

"Be careful. That one can sneak up on you." Tabitha grinned.

"I can tell." Miranda took yet another hefty bite.

"Tabitha's a remarkable pastry genius," Dominic praised. "Chase Confections desserts will be available here at Pearl during the anniversary month. They also ship made-to-order. But if you're ever in the D.C. area, be sure to visit Chase Confections. The bakery will be located just steps away from Shaw Hotel and Casino."

Tabitha listened as Dominic promoted both establishments with ease. The man was a natural.

She answered a few more questions while watching as Miranda tasted every item on the table, satisfying her sweet tooth. About fifteen minutes later, the camera crew of two broke down their equipment while Miranda and Dominic stood chatting a short distance away. As Tabitha cleaned her workstation and boxed up the pastries, she observed them from her periphery. Miranda's light touch on his forearm. The flirty laughter at something he said. Though they spoke in low tones, she could hear them making plans to get together again soon… *It's been too long.* Miranda's invitation came through loud as church bells, as did his reply. *That it has.*

She focused her attention on cleaning the table as the two approached her.

Miranda extended her hand. "It was a pleasure to meet you. I'll be sure to pay a visit to your bakery the next time I'm in D.C."

"We look forward to having you." More polite smiles.

Tabitha handed over three pastry-filled boxes. "Thought you all might like to take some desserts with you."

"Thank you." Miranda beckoned to the men, and they filed out on command behind her.

"That went well." Dominic snatched a cinnamon-sugar-dusted muffin and bit off practically half. "You did great," he said around a mouthful. "Tomorrow's interview with Ben Dunlevy should go similarly. I think you have it covered."

"Yep." Tabitha resumed cleaning. She was grouchy…and jealous. Without good reason. *Argh. Evie, why did you have to plant these thoughts about him in my head?*

"So, Miss Seils, what are your plans for later?" he asked before devouring the rest of the muffin.

"Work." She circled the table to the fridge to put away the rest of the uneaten desserts, then returned to finish tidying up. He trailed behind her and leaned his big body back against the table, his hands bracing the edge. "You're in the way." She nudged his frame and met resistance.

"I meant after work." He caught her wrist, his thumb stroking the pulse riding her vein, stalling her from scrubbing the metal surface.

Tabitha flashed her eyes to his but shuttered them briefly, shoving away her frustration along with her natural reaction to pull away. "It's my first day, and it'll be a long one. I need to keep an eye on things here, get a feel for the evening volume. I want to ensure everything is to my satisfaction. Now, if you don't mind, I have work to do."

"Take a walk with me. I think the place can survive without you for an hour. Besides, you have Andreas. And I'm sure Etienne could assist him if needed."

"I don't—"

"We won't even leave the hotel. One hour. What do you say? Are you going to make me beg? I will if that's what it'll take."

"That might be worth seeing." She couldn't contain a grin because his was broad and playful. "I guess I can spare an hour."

"Great."

She removed her chef jacket and hung it on a hook near her station. As she gave Andreas a few instructions, Dominic chatted with Etienne, whose gaze flickered to her with an assessing alertness.

She started toward the door. Dominic leaped forward and pushed it open, pinning himself against it.

"After you, Miss Seils." That grin of his was still flashing wickedly wide.

As they strode along, Tabitha asked, "What did you say to Etienne? He had a strange look."

"Just that you and I were headed to the suite to make mad, passionate love."

She stumbled, and her head snapped around. "You said what?" He looked at her for a long moment before his lips curled. Heat instantly rushed to her cheeks.

"Relax. I merely said we were going to grab a coffee."

Judging by Etienne's expression, Dominic likely said much more than that, but she didn't push it. She kept pace with his casual stride and couldn't help imagining them doing just that—stealing a quick tryst in the late afternoon as the sun hung above the Vegas skyline and broke through the bare windows, warming their already heated, naked flesh.

Would he fuck her quick and hard or take his time? *Both. Yes, both.* Wicked images of her beneath him, her on top, him behind her—"Oh!" She tripped over her own foot, heading face-first toward the tile, but strong arms caught her at the waist and pulled her back securely against the solid wall of his chest.

"Whoa! I got you."

She nodded rapidly while swallowing her embarrassment, then looked up over her shoulder at him. "I'm good." His warm palms splayed across her stomach, which somersaulted wildly.

"You're sure? Because I'd be happy to carry you." His voice held a soft, sexy, seducing sound.

His gaze dipped to her mouth. She instinctively moistened her lips. All it would take was for him to lower his head slightly and their lips would meet. Was he thinking about detouring to his suite? She sure the hell would be up for it. She untangled from his hold before she did something foolish, like attack his mouth with her own and grope the man right there in front of the horde of people moving to and fro. *What the hell is wrong with me?* She was so turned on by him all of a sudden.

"That won't be necessary. I'm good."

"If you insist." He released her, and they continued on.

Up ahead, a titanic, ivory statue of the goddess Athena beckoned guests with an elegantly extended hand into a replica of the Acropolis of ancient Greece. They crossed into the Parthenon where Doric marble columns separated a line of luxury boutiques, spas, and international eateries. The dome ceiling mirrored that of a natural, bright sunny sky with puffy white clouds that seemed to move as if on a gentle breeze. The sky-ceiling slowly dimmed, turning day into a full moon's glimmer of twinkling stars.

Tabitha stared up in awe and appreciation. "This is beautiful."

"Glad you approve. Trent and I designed it. Here we are." He led her into a small photography gallery.

"Mira, good afternoon."

A tall, slender woman hurried from behind a desk. "Dominic! So good to see you," she said in a Middle Eastern accent.

As the two hugged briefly, Tabitha hung back and surveyed the photography spotlighted on the walls. Dominic caught her hand, palmed the small of her back, and drew her forward.

"Mira, this is Tabitha Seils, owner of Chase Confections Bakery based out of D.C. She's at Pearl for the anniversary. Mira is the curator for Neal Blake."

Tabitha shook the woman's hand and returned a warm smile in kind. "The pictures are beautiful."

"Every item is a one-of-a-kind. The only difficult part about managing Mr. Blake's gallery is trying to decide which of his works to hang." A young couple entering hand in hand stole Mira's attention for a moment. She acknowledged them with slight nod.

"We're going to look around," Dominic said.

"I'm here if you have questions. Enjoy." She hurried on to assist the pair.

They moved about the gallery. One photo was lovelier than the next. Wildlife in its natural habitat. Images of beautiful landscapes and beaches from various corners around the world.

Dominic's head was angled and his unblinking gaze center-focused, studying, completely zoned in on a photo of a sun setting behind a rock formation.

"See how he captures the shadows, catching just enough light." He pointed at the photo, his stare transfixed.

It dawned on her. "The pictures in your suite, you took them." His stare shifted away from the photo and bored into her. "They're beautiful. You're really good."

"Thank you, but I'm no Neal Blake."

"I beg to differ. From what I saw, I think you're just as good, if not better."

Something flashed in his eyes before they moved on. He began explaining with an eagerness how the photographer, Blake, captured each image—the ISO level used. How the camera's f-stop determined the amount of light he let enter the lens. Though she didn't quite understand most of what he so easily described, Tabitha was drawn in by Dominic's knowledge of color, light, shadow, and angles. She was fascinated by his enthusiasm, intrigued by his passion, and completely turned on by the enjoyment she saw in his eyes.

"What?"

She blinked, realizing she'd been staring at his handsome face as he talked about a picture of an elephant with its young. "Nothing."

"Now that I've bored you for the past hour, I'll walk you back to Pearl."

She looked at her watch. *Damn.* "You haven't bored me. This was nice. I really enjoyed it." So much so, she found she didn't want to leave him just yet. "I believe, Mr. Balaska, you owe me a coffee."

His grin slid up slow and beautiful. "That I do."

They said a few words to Mira before leaving the gallery, crossed to a coffee bar a short distance away, and quickly placed their orders.

As Tabitha added a bit of cream to her cup, across the café table, Dominic stared at her in that all-consuming way he tended to have. "What is it? Do I have dough on my face? It wouldn't be the first time." She tried to make light of the scrutiny.

"Just enjoying the view. I'm snapping photos of you in my head."

His smiled wide and white and adorably sexy, the man had a strong charm about him, one Tabitha was discovering hard to ignore.

"Actually, I was wondering what you look like with your hair loose."

She straightened and ran a hand over her crown to the back of her perfect braid. "You got a problem with my hairstyle?"

"Not at all. You'd look beautiful sporting any style. It's just I've seen it only in a braid or pinned up."

It was the first compliment he'd ever given her.

During her chemo treatments, every strand had fallen out, even her eyebrows. Now she saw her hair as her lifeline—literally, a grand reassurance of her state of remission. She'd trimmed it an inch...maybe... in the last three and a half years but never more than that.

"Arranged like this, it stays out of the way while I work."

He sat forward with his arms crossed on the edge of the table. "So, Miss Seils, tell me about yourself. We've worked together on overseeing the construction for the bakery for nearly a year, but I don't feel I know you. Thanks to Etienne, I now know you're into rock climbing. And I discovered firsthand your appreciation for UFC when you laid me flat on my ass." He smirked.

It's a really nice ass. "I thought you were some naked, wacked-out-of-your-mind intruder. I mean, this is Vegas. How was I to know it was you?"

"Fair enough. Now, what else is there to know about you? With as much as you work, I presume you don't have any little ones at home."

He could ask that question again in six months and her answer might be altogether different. She took a sip of her coffee to settle the sudden anxious knot constricting in her stomach at the wonderful possibility, while eyeing him quizzically over the rim. How would he react if she shared that she might become a mom very soon? "The only babies I have are my two dwarf rabbits."

"Have you ever been married?"

"You're full of questions." She prickled.

"We're getting to know one another, remember?" He took her fisted hand that rested on the table and caressed his thumb slowly across her knuckles. "How about you ask me some questions. Whatever you like."

As he gently unfolded her fingers and slipped his hand in hers, a surprising calm rolled through her and the protective shield of wariness fell away. "I've never been married. How about you? Ever been married?"

"Nope."

"Are you and Celeste a couple?"

"We're no more a couple than you and Randy."

He still hadn't released her hand. "What about Valerie? Don't play me for a fool. You two have something going."

"She's made offers, but I swear to you my involvement with Valerie has been strictly business."

A sudden thump of contentment settled in her chest. "Do you have any kids?"

"Not one."

She shot him a sideways look. "Are you sure?"

"Absolutely sure." His thumb performed a slow stroking of her palm, back and forth, then moved up her wrist, sending a glorious shiver along her raised vein. With a soft grin, he leaned forward, his gaze steady. "I'm extremely careful, Miss Seils."

Her pulse thrummed, stealing her breath. "Do you see yourself having any kids? Better still, do you want any?" There was a slight pant in her speech, and she hoped he hadn't noticed.

"I've thought about it, but I'd be just as fine without them."

That wasn't an answer, but it wasn't a no either. *Promising.* With reluctance, she eased out of his hold and glanced at her watch. "I should get back to the restaurant."

"I'm late for a meeting, myself."

Her eyes widen. "Goodness, why didn't you say something?" She thrust out of her chair. "We didn't have to get coffee. You go on. I'll head back." She started off.

He came to his feet and caught her hand. "Slow down. I

have people in place who can handle things in my absence. Besides, this was more important. Come here." He drew her closer. "I wanted this time with you." The light touch of fingers tucked unruly strands behind her ear.

Tabitha's heart pounded with a ferocious shudder. "And why is that?" She took a step closer, holding his suddenly hooded gaze, wanting to put her hands on him in all the right ways.

"Like I've said before, I think we got off on the wrong foot." He narrowed the space even more as the atmosphere between them seemed to shift, crackling with heat. "I'd like to start over. Think we can do that?"

"We can do that."

A satisfied smile played about his features. "After you, Miss Seils."

She led the way and hoped she wasn't misreading the *connection*.

Chapter Ten

TABITHA ENTERED THE dark hotel suite and headed straight for the TV remote. She wanted to catch Miranda Edwards's news segment. The time at the bottom of the screen flashed 10:21 as the meteorologist forecast more Vegas sunny skies with low humidity. *Damn it.* Miranda's piece had come and gone.

The city lights looming through the windows guided her trek to the bathroom. She stripped, unbraided her hair, and stepped beneath the rain showerhead, letting the weight of the day slide down the drain.

Slipping on a cotton tank and panties, she wrapped herself in her robe, then headed back into the living room. A photo of a beautiful sunset on the wall caught her eye. Beside it was one of a breathtakingly gorgeous sunrise. There were several artfully framed pictures of cityscapes and beach scenes with different depictions of dusk and dawn hanging all around the space. Dominic really had a knack for photography, likely more than he even realized. Each picture championed his talent.

She found herself at the door of his bedroom and hesitated for only a moment before flipping the wall switch that turned on the bedside lamp. His dark suit lay thrown across the chaise longue. A bath towel on the floor. Black leather dress shoes near the bench stationed at the foot of the bed—the entire outfit she'd seen him in earlier today. Apparently, he'd been in the suite to change at some point.

Where was he tonight…and with whom? *Miranda.* If he was out with the reporter, Tabitha had severely misread him this afternoon over coffee. She wished it didn't matter, but it did. She'd lowered her guard a rung to let him in. With unexpected emotions crowding her throat, she turned off the TV and went to bed.

The room was pitch-black with the shades drawn, just the way she liked it, yet she couldn't fall asleep.

I wanted this time with you… I'd like to start over.

She tore apart each word, analyzing his slightest touch and simplest expression. Could she have been so far off the mark?

The clock crawled close to 10:50. Every sound sparked her anticipation—Dominic had returned—only for it not to be so. She got up, threw on her workout gear, and left the suite. A few laps on the treadmill might help to clear her head.

The elevator doors parted. Weston returned a wave from his perch at the concierge counter on her way across the lobby.

The exercise room was much larger than the typical cramped quarters found in most hotels. It had all the latest and greatest equipment, and surprisingly, it was packed. She snatched a fresh towel from a folded stack on the table and made a beeline for the one unoccupied treadmill. With the speed cranked at her usual max, skipping a warm-up, she dug her heels in quick and deep.

After a good forty minutes of running on a steep incline, working the tension in her muscles, she slowed and stepped off. Her legs were on fire. Sweat ran down her skin in salty streams, soaking her clothes. Strands of wet hair clung to her hot face. She gulped from her water bottle to relieve the dryness in her throat and the convulsing in her stomach while wiping down the equipment with the supplied disinfectant.

"You went hard on that run."

Tabitha spun, hitching a breath. Dominic stood before her. Moisture exaggerated the waves in his dark hair. His sleeveless shirt hugged the sweat-glistening bulges of his upper body. Loose fitting shorts and well-used athletic sneakers completed his workout apparel. "You're here?"

He laughed. "You sound surprised. Where did you expect me to be?"

With the reporter. "I meant, I didn't know you were here."

"I was stretched out on the weight bench when you came in. You seemed on a mission the way you rushed that machine and beat the shit out of it," he said around a chuckle. "I wasn't about to get in the way."

She laughed lightly on a comfortingly relaxed ripple and looked around. "I hadn't expected it would be this crowded. I couldn't sleep. Thought a run would help. And you? It's late."

"I had a full day. It's the only time I had."

Silence hung a moment. She was still working through her glee of surprise. "Well, I'll let you get back—"

"I'm finished."

"Me too." They started forward and left the facility.

Once again Weston offered up an acknowledging smile on their way past him to the private elevators. Her phone dinged as she and Dominic stepped aboard. She sent off a delayed reply to her friends' nightly group text. When she looked up, Dominic's gaze was pinned on her in the mirrored doors.

"Kennedi and Evie said hello."

He nodded, his expression no less bold.

The doors parted, and he beckoned her to lead but crossed the short distance and swiped his card at the door.

The cool, dark space sent voluminous shivers down Tabitha's damp spine as apprehension assaulted her belly. *See something.* "Would you like something to drink?" Shit, she was so rusty at this. "If I were home, I'd whip us up a kale smoothie."

"Rain check, then. I'm going to shower. Hope you sleep well."

"You too. Good night." At her bedroom door, she gave a look over her shoulder; he'd done the same. Both returned subtle nods, then he disappeared within.

She went into the bathroom, stripped, and paced the tile. Ten, maybe twelve broad steps would put her at his door. She could deny her caution.

Contemplation waged a war inside her; she didn't trust her judgment.

What would it feel like to have his lips pressed against hers and his large, strong hands exploring her body?

Stop it. She started her shower and hastily stepped beneath the cool spray to stave her lust. Then cranked the temperature to as hot as her skin could stand.

A formidable knock came at the door. Startled, taking a breath, then another, she responded, "Yes?"

"Mind if I join you?"

A fierce shudder rushed through her. *Hell yes!* She grinned and did a light tap of feet upon the wet tile, then sobered. "Come in." Through the rapid fog of the glass, Dominic stood before her, all sleekly muscled, beautifully naked, and exceptionally hard.

Sweet mercy.

She pushed open the shower door. "I said, come in."

He joined her under the rain shower. A strong hand fitted her hip, scorching her already heated flesh. The other roped around her drenched braid, tugging lightly. "Are you sure? There's still time to change your mind."

As if she had that level of fortitude. "It's been over a year. Trust me, I'm sure." She slipped her fingers in his soaked hair and pulled him down to the crush of her greedy mouth. Her tongue instantly snaked within. Soft. Sweet.

He devoured her lips, her neck, her breasts, and back to her mouth with frantic urgency as he pressed her against the smooth tiles, pinning her with the power of his body. She clung to the solid slickness of his muscled shoulders as her lust for him coursed like a tidal wave, near desperate to be slaked.

Both almost lost their footing on the slippery surface as they began groping and exploring their hot, wet flesh. With surprising speed, he gripped and lifted her by the buttocks, left the shower, crossed the room, and came down with her on her bed. As he ferociously took her mouth, his hand went between her legs. Skillful fingers toyed with her overly sensitive sex, stroking deep, over and over, sending her mind and body on a soaring, pleasurable high. He halted his urgent kisses, his breath labored, yet his fingers in her pussy kept up their sweet caresses.

"I need to get a condom. I didn't expect you'd invite me in."

She drew back. "You came to me naked with this kickass body on display, sporting the most beautiful erection I've seen in a long time, and you expected I'd say no?"

His lips quirked. "In fairness, I left my shorts at the door. When you answered, I felt I stood a chance, so I went for it. I'll be right back." He left the bed and jetted out of the room. Mere seconds later, with his shaft fully gloved, he tossed a strip of condoms on the nightstand before joining her upon the damp sheets.

His knees parted her thighs with lascivious intention as his lips met hers, their tongues mating and exploring in slow swirls. When he entered her, taking her in teasingly unhurried increments, an unforgiving "yes" fell from her slightly parted lips. Soon, he began pounding into her with a reckless rush, a fierce joining of bodies.

"Dominic, I want to have you my way," she whispered against his mouth.

He drew back, breath shallow, eyes hooded, chuckling. "It would surprise me if you didn't." His large hands cradled her face. "You can have me any way you like, Miss Boss Lady." He touched the soft cushion of his mouth to hers, his kisses so surprisingly tender.

Tabitha coaxed him onto his back and straddled his hips. His eyes shuttered as she took him in fully, her inner muscles squeezing, then reached back, gripped his thigh, anchoring her position, and rode his cock. Hips undulating, pumping. Carnal, demanding, and she was more than a little shocked by how much she craved him. She closed her eyes to savor the pulsing feel of him so deep inside her, easing to small lifts and determined grinds as she slid him out of her to the very tip of madness, repeating it again and again.

His eyes stayed fixed on hers as his hands cupped and toyed with her breasts, his touch excruciatingly light, thumbs brushing her nipples that were already taut and achy. And when he lifted his head and captured one stiff peak between his lips, sucking hard, Tabitha nearly shattered into a thousand pieces from the pleasure it provoked.

He caught her buttocks in both hands, pitching her forward, and thrust rapidly, repeatedly, claiming her body with his commanding plunges. She met his urgency with wild abandon, sending their bodies into a fierce surge of spasms.

She collapsed her full weight upon his sweaty, heaving chest as their breaths came in quick, choppy snatches. When her nerve endings fired back up and she could feel her toes again, she rolled off him onto her back.

The air-conditioning clicked on, filling the room with much-needed comfort. For long minutes, they lay quiet, stretched out atop rumpled sheets, letting the coolness dry their sweat-soaked bodies.

"Over a year, huh?"

She turned her head to him. Both started to chuckle.

Tabitha reached to the nightstand and grabbed another

condom. Smiling, she held it up. "It's been a long time."

And he didn't disappoint—the feel of him above her, inside her, taking back the control with his kiss, his touch. She cupped his firm buttocks; her hips followed his rhythm until their panting breaths were rough, throwing them into another hot, sweaty blissful crescendo.

TABITHA'S PHONE CHIRPED a symphony of birds, drawing her from a heavy sleep. Five a.m. had come far too quickly.

She pulled the device from underneath her pillow and tapped off the alarm, then buried her face in the comfort of thick memory foam, stealing precious minutes.

A click of the remote raised the shades a touch. Dominic's silhouette lying beside her skimmed the shadows. His deep, even breathing confirmed that her alarm hadn't disturbed his slumber. No surprise. When she'd finally let him up for air, fatigue had settled over the man's well-used, satiated body like a weighted anchor, sinking him almost instantly into unconsciousness.

Apprehension shoved aside her cloud of euphoria. She didn't want to read more into their night of mind-blinking amazing sex. She'd hold her feelings in shielded check for now.

She eased out of bed, gathered her things, and went to his bathroom to shower.

Dressed, she headed to work.

Chapter Eleven

"Miss Seils, we should get started."

Tabitha looked over her shoulder at the reporter, who'd been patiently waiting, then across the kitchen at the entrance. Though Dominic had replied to her text, saying he wouldn't be joining her for the interview, she'd been so certain of the contrary. He'd come striding through the door in that "no particular hurry" way he moved and that only he could make look sexy. She'd even made his favorite blueberry scones, adding extra bourbon butter. But he was a man of his word.

"Miss Seils?"

She sat down on the metal stool facing Mr. Dunlevy and gave a small smile. "Where should I start?"

With his notepad in hand, evidently going about the interview old school, he gestured at the layout of pastries upon the table. "Tell me about Chase Confections. Everything looks delicious."

When he reached for the scones, she subtly slid the dish back and brought forward the raspberry-lemon tarte au soleil as she talked up the confectionary. Around a half hour later and after Mr. Dunlevy had scarfed down a good bit of the samplers, he put his pen and pad into his worn leather satchel—Tabitha's cue the interview had come to a close— and came to his feet. She quickly boxed up the remaining baked goods along with the untouched scones and handed the desserts off to Mr. Dunlevy on his way out.

With Andreas's help, she spent the rest of the day in routine mode, preparing desserts for the busy restaurant.

Etienne popped over now and again to check in, but running the kitchen kept him otherwise occupied. Though he and his staff were convivial, Friday couldn't come fast enough. She was ready to return home. The last thing she needed was wondering, hoping, wishing a guy was interested in her. Throw in sex and it only mounted the complications.

Blueberry with goat cheese pie was the specialty dessert of the day. Not that she'd chosen it on the off chance Dominic would stop by, but because it'd been rated top of the list in the table survey. *Shit. Who am I kidding?*

When she made it back to the hotel suite that evening, after a quick sprint at the gym, alone in the cool space, she huddled on the couch in her robe, flipping through the nightly news while Dominic was MIA. *It was one night of great sex. Get over it. Evidently he's not sitting around panting over it.*

Her cell phone ringing on the center table pulled her out of a comfortable slough. It was closing in on one o'clock in the morning, East Coast time. Troy must be on night rotation at the firehouse. She opened the line.

"Hey. Slow night?"

"A slow night is a good night in my line of work. Is there something you want to tell me, sis?"

"What?"

"I got a voicemail message from a Marylin Winslow with the Parker Adoption Agency asking to schedule a sit-down with me for an interview. She said it's in reference to you adopting a kid. What is this about?"

Tabitha winced. They'd already moved on to family. It was too fast considering she'd only sent the completed paperwork to the agency minutes before leaving for Vegas. What if Kaitlyn had the baby prematurely? The total fees would then become due just as premature. Neonatal costs were no doubt steep. Would that increase the monetary requirement, too? Her mind flooded with scenarios that stirred her anxiety.

"Tabitha?"

"It's just what it is. I've decided to adopt. Interviewing family and close friends is part of the process."

"Adopting a kid is a lot to take on. I mean, you're at the bakery from sunup to sundown. How are you going to squeeze in caring for a kid?"

"You forget I was once pregnant," she bristled. "The same responsibilities apply."

"Sis, I know." His tone grew soft. "Tabby, with everything that happened, all you went through, I'm only saying you should really think about it. Maybe focus on your business. That's a full-time gig in itself."

Tabitha didn't want to be reminded of the awful past, nor was she in the mood to argue about her present choices. "Troy, please return Ms. Winslow's call."

"Do Mom and Dad know?"

"No, but if the agency contacted you, I'm sure they'll get a call soon."

"There's no way you told John. I would've heard from him on this."

She feared telling her eldest brother more than her parents. "I intend to call everyone."

"Well, it does explain why I got a vibe. I knew something was up with you. What'cha getting into out there in Vegas?"

Her twin could always sense when she wasn't up to par.

"Just relaxing. The restaurant's been keeping me busy."

"Hope you're finding time to see the city. You're in Vegas. You know what they say."

"Of course. What happens in Vegas—"

"No, more like YOLO. Sis, you work hard, so play a little. No doubt a party is happening somewhere. Hell, likely right there at Shaw's."

Tabitha looked down at her state of dress and around the spacious suite. She was a party of one. "I have an early start tomorrow. Besides, I'm only here till Friday." She put the call on speaker, then retrieved a hotel flyer from the side table that advertised all of the events scheduled for the anniversary month. There were indeed parties, concerts, and events going on practically every day and into the night. It was likely where Dominic was spending his evening.

"Tabby, you know how much I could get into in three days? You better dig your heels into Sin City, get your party on." He chuckled, then a long breath release followed. "Seriously, you okay? Like I said, I got the itch to check up on my baby sis."

He was a mere seven minutes older. Tabitha's eyes were drawn to the picture that hung to the right of the flat screen. The sunset crowning a cerulean sea was so breathtakingly beautiful it made her want to dive right in. All of the photography art in the room, even the one of a severe storm with its overturned vehicles and mature trees bent nearly sideways, held a tragic appeal.

"Tabby, you there?"

She blinked. "I'm here. There's this gu—" Her head swung in the direction of the entry door. Was that the click of the lock? Dominic entered and paused midstride. His brow knitted tightly enough to concern her. "I'll call you when I get back. Love you." She stuck her phone into the pocket of her robe and came to her feet. "Hey."

"Evening." He continued toward his bedroom, shrugging out of his suit jacket. "Don't let me stop your pillow talk. You didn't have to hang up with the dude on my account." His tone was about as chilly as his glacial blues. And why assume it was a man she'd been talking to after sharing her bed just the night before? She didn't know how to take that.

"It's not—" Something was very wrong. They weren't a couple to the extent that she should expect him to confide in her. Instead, she followed him and stood just inside his room as he sat on the bench at the foot of the bed and removed his shoes. "Busy day?" The hint of nicotine wafted her nose from his jacket tossed onto the chaise.

"Yeah," he all but grunted.

"Same here. The interview went well. I added a few new desserts to the sampler. Etienne liked—" She paused when he got up and went into his closet, then came out in his undershirt and slacks, hardly giving her a glance as he crossed to the bathroom. She stayed in step behind him and leaned a shoulder against the doorjamb, trying her best to appear impervious to his cold demeanor. "I was saying…" He drew his T-shirt over his head, grabbed the shampoo from the wall niche, then started the shower, as if she wasn't even there. "Damn it, Dominic, can you just stop for a minute? I'm trying to talk to you!"

He faced her. "Yeah, what is it?" A condescending mildness. His disinterest in her and anything she had to say was clearly conveyed.

"You know what, forget it. I don't know what changed between last night and now, but whatever. You do you." If he wanted to close her off, fine. She pivoted and started out of the room.

"Wait. Tabitha?" He caught her hand, drawing her to a stop, but let go when she tugged. "I'm sorry." As his thumb caressed her cheek, a sudden seriousness crept into his expression. "I had a very shitty day that only got worse this evening, but it's no excuse to take it out on you." He tipped her chin up and pressed a soft kiss on her lips.

"You smell as if you've been in a tobacco factory. I thought this was a smoke-free hotel."

"The hotel is smoke free. I was on the casino side tonight. The man I had a meeting with kept a stick lit." He took her hand and came in for another kiss. "Join me, beautiful."

A feral light now glowed in his heavy-lidded gaze as she undid his belt, unzipped his pants, and hooked her thumbs at his waistband then paused and smiled. "I've already showered. When you're done, I'll have a glass of wine waiting. I want to try that Stag's Leap Cask 23. I got to tour their vineyard some years ago." She backed away and left the room before succumbing to her desire to take him up on his offer.

From her seventy-two-story tower, she looked out the window at the Technicolor lights. The tallest structures on the Strip, Shaw Hotel and Casino sat at the crest of the bustling skyline. When she'd arrived, the demigod Triton's white marble statue, which stood tall and intimidatingly beautiful within a royal-blue water feature, greeted her on the drive leading to the grand entrance. A trident rode the side of the building in a soft shadowy silhouette. It'd reminded her of Gotham's Bat-Signal. To think her best friend was about to marry into all of this—

Hearing light footsteps, she turned. Dominic came out of the room. He wore a simple T-shirt and loose shorts. Freshly shampooed hair formed exaggerated waves at the crown of his head.

She crossed to the kitchen.

"I got it." He opened and poured the rich cabernet sauvignon. With filled wineglasses in hand, they moved to the couch.

Tabitha took a sip. "Hmm, this is really good."

"At three fifty a bottle, it better be," he remarked before taking a swallow from his glass.

She gaped. "What? Shit, why didn't you say something?"

"It's not an issue. You wanted it, so we'll drink it. Whatever you wish, Miss Seils." He tipped his head to her.

She took a large gulp, intending to suck down every dollar, and relaxed back, facing him. "Now, tell me about this shitty day of yours."

He exhaled heavily. "An investment deal I tried to put

together fell through."

"What sort of investment deal, if you don't mind me asking?"

"One where I wouldn't need to rely on my trust. I'd be free to do my own thing."

Tabitha angled her head. "You have a trust fund, but would rather seek investment instead of using your own money?"

"I don't have access to it. Well, I would if I got hitched." The defined angle in his jaw flexed.

Still not quite following, she waited for him to finish his swallow. "Are you saying you have to get married in order to get your trust?"

"I have to *be* married by age thirty-one. Oh, and have a kid the first year of wedded bliss to fully satisfy the trust clause."

Her eyes widened. She stared into his calm ones. "Seriously?"

"Yep."

"Who would write such a ridiculous agreement?"

He finished off his glass, then jogged to the kitchen and grabbed the bottle from the counter. "You'd have to talk to the Greeks of old," he said on his return to the couch and refilled his glass before topping off hers. "The trust doc has been in my family for generations. I'm told it was written that way so the Balaska name would forever carry forward." A rough chuckle. "The bastards were cunning, for sure."

"When do you turn thirty-one? And what happens to the money if you don't meet the deadline?"

"December seventh. The funds get forfeited back to the

trust. My sister can attest to that. For the women in the family, they have to meet the clause by age twenty-five. Her husband, then boyfriend was stationed overseas and couldn't get leave. She was given no exceptions."

Six months. What in all hell…? It was as though a truck had slammed into her. She looked away from his even gaze and took several deep gulps of her wine, emptying the glass to resuscitate and regulate her racing heartbeat. He could very well be married in six months. Hell, and even have a baby. She bit the inside of her jaw to tamp down the distress of knowing she could never compete with that.

"My meeting this evening was to seek private money to join in a condo project Trent's got going in Dubai. But like I said, it fell through. I also wanted the funds for another purpose. I'd like to open a photography gallery. And perhaps start a photography school. I guess one day."

Tabitha followed his now-solemn gaze to the picture hanging next to the flat screen. "That one is my favorite. You really have a gift." It was clearly his true passion and was quite obvious what he really wanted to do. "What about Trent? Maybe he could help with the Dubai funds you need."

"Between his percentage already tied up in the Dubai partnership, the D.C. casino construction underway, as well as a small real estate project he has going in Chicago and added to it his financial involvement with Kennedi's father's company, Trent's stretched pretty tight." He finished off his wine and sat the glass on the side table, then scooted closer. "Enough talk about my exceptionally shitty day. Besides, with you here, it's looking a lot better." A soft grin played across his lips as his hand slipped beneath her robe and skated slowly up her inner thigh. The tips of his fingers skimmed her sex through her satin panties. "Picturing you naked got me through my day."

Heat instantly pooled at her apex, her arousal striking in quick pulses. She tried to keep a level head. "Sure, Balaska. If you say so."

"You were." He moved to his knees on the plush area rug and came in between her legs. "This is what I imagined doing to you." His strong hands expertly worked her arches, over her ankles, massaged the tightness in her calves, and along the firm curves of her thighs. It felt heavenly.

Tabitha closed her eyes on a sigh. "You're extremely good at that."

He parted her robe. An index finger traced her ink along the raised skin. "What happened here?"

She inched away from his inquisitive touch. She hated that scar. It was a stark reminder that having a child might not be in the cards for her. It was the reason she'd gotten the tattoo to cover it. That way, at the very least, she didn't have to look at it.

"It's nothing."

Though there was still a questioning look in his gaze, he brought his mouth to her ink, and trailed slow, warm kisses along the pattern. Her stomach fluttered nervously. Jeff had never done that. He'd once said the scar marred an otherwise perfect body. It'd been a joke, he'd stressed, but she knew he meant it. Being made to feel ugly and overall self-conscious were among the many other reasons she'd gotten the tattoo.

"Ivy is my middle name."

He looked up. "Savino's mine, since we're sharing. I guess that explains it. Not completely, but I'll let it go. I have a confession to make," he added, wearing a crooked smirk.

"What is it?"

"I often fantasize about you."

Tabitha willed herself not to blush and sucked her teeth. "Sure you do." In truth, his words gave her warm chills. "If you do, I highly doubt I'm the only one."

"You are."

She rolled her eyes at him in utter disbelief.

"It's true. Among other things, here's what I'm doing to you in my fantasy." Slowly, he glided his hands up her thighs, over her hips, to her breasts, cupped and caressed. He kissed and nipped the column of her neck, drawing out a soft gasp she couldn't contain. "And this." Clever fingers slipped beneath the string of her thong, two thick digits filling her sex, tunneling, stretching, pumping slowly, again and again.

"Dominic, we…we…" Her eyes shuttered on a breathy pant at the swift surge of excruciating pleasure, barely hanging on to self-control.

His tongue brushed across her parted lips, featherlight, taunting as his fingers continued a measured thrusting. "Right there?" he whispered against her mouth.

She nodded, unable to focus, near delirious with need, her raw hunger for him clawing at her insides. Her eyes fluttered open at the sound of him shoving the center table back. In a flash, he wrenched the delicate satin down her legs and pressed his mouth to the triangle of her mound. His tongue snaked between the slit of her folds and flicked her throbbing clit, chipping away at her lustful craving. He tugged off her panties the rest of the way, brought her legs over his shoulders, and with both hands on her buttocks, dragged her forward to the edge of the couch. His mouth clamped on, his tongue swirling and licking her clit while two fingers reentered her pussy, working her without mercy.

She moaned his name, unable to stifle the soft cry that tore from her throat as he found sweet spot after sweet spot. Every angle his fingers and tongue toured drove her hotter until all she could focus on was the wild rush toward that precipice of heightened pleasure, riding the wave with mindless abandon. Her sex clenched. Her back arched sharply. She threw her head back as her orgasm struck with thunderous force. Her eyes fluttered open to see him give one final, long stroke of his tongue.

"Are you convinced now, Miss Seils?" His eyes were heavy, his breathing ragged, the evidence of his unquenched need apparent by the bulge in his shorts.

"Yes," she said on a hoarse whisper. *Goodness, yes!*

He came to his feet. She followed on unsteady limbs. The man's tongue and fingers marveled like none other.

"That was…" She shook the haze from her ruffled brain. When he eased her robe off her shoulders, she shuddered as his warm lips skimmed the hollow of her collarbone, following along the contours of her throat, and up to claim her mouth. He delivered a kiss, a long, tongue-stroking so hot and greedy, it was her undoing. She yanked at the band of his shorts, prepared to repay the pleasure, but he caught her behind the knees and scooped her into his arms.

"I'm not done with you," he said on his stroll to his bedroom. "That *yes* didn't sound sure enough. I think you need more convincing."

His grin was sinfully wicked, and he convinced her over and over and over.

Chapter Twelve

T HE MORNING FLEW by. Tabitha had been on overdrive from the moment she entered the kitchen at six a.m., almost mechanical in her movements. With Andreas's help, there were enough dessert items prepped for the evening peak time, and it was only three in the afternoon.

She'd been warned Thursday was usually the day the high-dollar clientele rolled in and to expect it to get quite crazy with special requests. Those patrons typically took their meals in their private suites. The hotel and restaurant catered to their every whim.

Tabitha dried her hands on a towel and hung it over her shoulder while pulling her ringing cell from her back pocket.

"Hi, Mom."

"Hello, sweetheart. What is this about you adopting a child? I received a call from a Parker Adoption. You're being screened. Why am I just hearing about this?"

She bit down on her bottom lip. "I was going to call you. I've been busy. I've actually been working in Vegas this week." The timer beeped. She propped the phone between her cheek and shoulder to pull the cake from the oven. Andreas stepped up without fail to assist. She gave him an approving grin, then headed to Etienne's office and closed the door. "Yes, it was sudden, but—"

"Are you sure this is a good idea? Your father and I don't think it's wise."

Just like her friends. "Well, it's what I—"

"Tabby, I saw what your miscarriage did to your spirit. Losing a child is devastating, but adopting a child to replace the one you lost—"

Tears instantly stung the back of her throat. "That's not the case." But she could no longer say for sure and now understood where all the opposition stemmed from. "Look, I can't get into this right now."

"I'm only saying this is a big decision that shouldn't be taken lightly. You won't be able to run off to Vegas at the drop of a hat for work or otherwise with a baby at home."

Tabitha closed her eyes and stroked the sudden throb at her right temple. "Mom, John's calling. I'll come by when I get back."

"You do that, sweetheart. But think about what I said. Love you."

"Love you too." She disconnected but didn't take her brother's call. Unlike Troy, who wanted to see her get back out and date, John wanted to tuck her away, protect her from even the slightest scrape. She didn't need another lecture.

On her way back to the kitchen, her phone rang again. *Dominic.* An uncharacteristic lurch assaulted her belly. He'd pleasured her so thoroughly and completely, she still hadn't recovered and could almost feel his hands moving along her fevered skin, his fingers lightly, teasingly brushing the underside of her breasts. His thumbs toying with her nipples until they were stiff and achy. Tabitha swallowed hard and opened the line but kept her tone mild. "Afternoon."

"Hey, beautiful. How's your day going?"

She smiled like a giddy schoolgirl, her spirits lifted instantly. "Busy, but okay. You?"

"Fine. I'm attending an event tonight. If you care to join me, you'll need to be ready by eight. Sharp."

Perhaps this was his unpolished way of asking her out on a date. "What type of event is it?"

"The champagne and caviar type. Investors and business associates are in town for Shaw's anniversary. For you, it's a networking opportunity to get your company's name out there. The event's held in the Sea Glass lounge downstairs. Oh, and it's black tie. If that's a problem for you—"

"It's not." *Okay, not a date.* Relieved or disappointed? Choosing the latter… "I'll be ready."

"Until then, enjoy your day."

"You too." He'd sounded all business. Tabitha called Andreas over and let him know she'd be leaving early. She gave him a few instructions before dialing the concierge. The line connected almost instantly.

"Shaw Hotel. Weston Perez. How may I assist you, Miss Seils?"

"I need to purchase a really nice dress for a formal event tonight. Any recommendations on where I might do that?"

DOMINIC PAUSED IN perfecting his bow tie to catch his cell phone ringing on the bed. He anticipated his brother's routine evening call to check in.

"Hey."

"How were things at the office? No fires to tackle, I hope?"

"None that I couldn't handle." He returned to the full-length mirror.

"And Tabitha? All's good with her and Etienne?"

"From what I can tell, yes. She and I are headed to a party tonight."

"You two going on a date?" Trenton's voice perked up.

"It's not a date." Until Dominic figured out himself what he and Tabitha were doing, he didn't feel it necessary to share more with his brother. Especially since he'd been told Tabitha was off-limits—although that was when it came to settling his trust. "It's an opportunity for her to promote Chase Confections. Isn't that the point of her being here?"

"Yes, but it's also an opportunity for you two to find comfortable ground without bickering all the time."

Dominic snorted. "I knew it was the real reason you had her come instead of your fiancée or Evie."

"Yes, it was. Now, don't change the subject. Do you want tonight to be a date with Tabitha?"

"Damn, dude. You're starting to sound like Mom. Cool it with the matchmaking. I have to hear it enough from her. How are things in Dubai?"

"Good. All of the investors are still in play. I've held off on finalizing the agreement in case you get your trust settled and are able to participate."

"Yes, well, I don't see that happening." Dominic checked his watch. "We should've left nearly an hour ago."

"Where's Tabitha?"

"In her room. What the hell is she doing in there? How hard can it be to shower, throw on an outfit and a pair of shoes?"

Trenton laughed. "Clearly you've never lived with a woman. More to the point, you've never had to wait patiently on one to dress for an event." More chuckles. "I'll catch up with you tomorrow."

"Later." Dominic stuck the phone in his pants pocket and left the bedroom. With a glance at his watch again, he crossed to Tabitha's door and delivered a firm rap on it. "Hey, we need to get going." He could hear what sounded like the hair dryer shut off.

"I'm almost ready."

Almost? *Are you kidding me!* "What's tak—?" The door opened.

Holy fuck! The sight of her stole Dominic's will to breathe. Voluminous curls draped her bare shoulders, long and fluid, hitting at the waist. The dress gave him a tease of smooth, toned thighs. Firm calves flowed down to red, severely high-heeled strappy scandals. She flicked the hair dryer back on, bent forward, head lowered, and rustled her fingers in the thick tresses, assisting the warm air through the strands, then stood.

Wow…

"My hair takes forever to dry. And my zipper's stuck. I think it's caught on the fabric. Mind giving me a hand?" She turned around and drew the copious locks forward over her shoulder, exposing the partial opening of her dress. The strapless, red sequin number lay so perfectly over the soft contour of her tawny skin.

She looked over her shoulder, heavy winged lashes canopying those enchanting hazel eyes. "Well, can you fix it?"

What the fuck was wrong with him? He hadn't moved, overcome by the rapid pulse pounding away in his chest. "Uh, sure." He stepped in close behind her. The scent of fresh berries tickled his nose. He found he wanted to explore the sweet fragrance of her hair and the intoxicatingly pleasant perfume of her body but forced himself to concentrate on the task at hand. "It's caught."

She looked back again on a light chuckle with a perfectly arched eyebrow raised, cherry-colored lips curved. "Is it now?"

Dominic had never discounted she was a beautiful woman. He found her bold and jagged-edge sexy. That fuck-off-I-have-shit-to-do attitude she wore like a badge no doubt pushed away most men on purpose. But tonight, she'd be impossible to ignore.

"I need to unzip to release the fabric."

"Okay, but be careful not to rip it."

The backs of his fingers grazed silky smooth, warm flesh as he was careful not to tear the dress. "I think I got it." A light tug freed the material. "There." He filled his palms with her hair merely because he'd imagined doing it numerous times, sliding his hands down the long mane, allowing the heavy tresses to drape gently over her slender spine.

"Thanks." She grabbed her purse from the bed, then turned to face him. "We're late, I know. Sorry. I decided to get a French mani-pedi. It took longer than I expected." She held up a hand, putting on display blunt, white-tipped, polished nails and stuck out a foot.

He leaned in and nuzzled her neck. "I want to taste every inch of your skin." The sudden urge struck strong, feral.

"Later for that, big boy. We're late, remember?"

"I'll be envied tonight." Her rare smile consumed him.

"You're wearing that tux pretty well yourself. Oh, I almost forgot." She set her purse on the nightstand and started fiddling with the tiny diamond stud at the side of her nose.

"What are you doing?"

"Removing my nose ring. The party being black tie and all, I wouldn't want—"

"Don't!" He liked the subtle sparkle it gave to an already perfect canvas. The tattoo and the nose ring were contrary to the arid demeanor she tended to project. "You forget it's Vegas. Besides, the crowd tonight is relatively loose for the most part. We should go. There's someone I'd like to try to get in front of. Hope he's still around. He doesn't plan to be here long, if at all."

"Then we better go."

TABITHA STEPPED OFF the packed elevator with Dominic behind her. "So, which way is the Sea Glass lounge?"

"It's within the casino, which is past the sculpture garden."

"And where's the sculpture garden?"

His eyes widened a touch. "You haven't been to the garden? There are those who come here for the sole purpose of gambling, of course, but a good number of tourists seek out the garden of the Greek gods."

"I get it now. You're Greek. That explains why Trent has the Triton, son of Poseidon, as his logo. Makes sense."

He gave a nod. "Trent had the garden—the statues—created as a gift to our mother. She's heavily into Greek mythology. She's also obsessed with our family's genealogy and has traced our lineage as far back as 1760. Heritage is everything, she likes to say," he muttered with a slight eye roll.

Choosing not to delve more into it, she looked out at the forever-crowded lobby. "Well, Mr. Balaska, lead the way." They strode past the concierge. She sent Weston a thumbs-up in response to his smile and silent *well done*. The dress, shoes, and clutch cost a small fortune but were worth it.

"What was that about?" Dominic asked. "You two friends now?"

"We were never enemies." Tabitha cut a glance up at him. He made a peculiar face. Merely quizzical or bothered, she couldn't quite tell. "Weston came through for me today on something. If you recall, he even arranged accommodations for me after you failed to book me a room."

"I did reserve your room, Miss Seils. There was a mix-up with the reservation." He continued in hard clips across the polished ecru-tiled floor. A sudden pivot, and he caught her wrist.

Tabitha stopped short, nearly running into him. "What? I was only teasing. You have a pretty cool setup here. Big penthouse suite. Maid service twice a day. I noticed today someone had even stocked the fridge with every juice imaginable."

His arm hooked her waist, reeling her in against his side. "I like to think it turned out okay." He tipped her chin up for a light peck on the lips, not caring about those who had to skirt around them to get past. "Would you agree?" he murmured against her mouth.

"Very much." She grinned.

He released his hold, and they continued across the lobby.

The burn in her airways from the cloud of nicotine came swiftly as they entered the casino side of the hotel. They stepped before a staffer at the entrance to the Sea Glass lounge.

"ID, please. It's a private party," the man requested, his attention on the electronic pad in his hand, repeatedly stabbing a finger on the display. "The screen's frozen." He looked up. His eyes widened. "Oh! Mr. Balaska." He hastily pulled open the door to reveal a decent-sized crowd. "Sorry, sir."

"No harm done," Dominic answered with a sedate grin as they crossed the threshold.

The Sea Glass was a surround of rubbed brass fixtures, polished, dark mahogany gaming tables, and royal-blue, crushed-velvet seating. Along the far wall, aquatic life swam within the floor-to-ceiling aquarium. Bartenders dressed in tuxedos pulled top-tier bottles from the glass shelves behind them in quick succession. Over in the corner, atop a raised plinth, the pianist's nimble fingers moved along the ebony and ivory keys of a black-lacquer grand piano. Waiters circled the room, carrying silver trays of drinks and hors d'oeuvres. It was a refined space of elegance and sophistication for those ready to dabble in high stakes.

"Food. Great, I'm starved." Dominic caught the sleeve of a passing waiter. "My man. What do you have here?"

"Beef yakitori skewers." The waiter handed over a napkin.

"That'll work." Dominic took two skewers and offered one to Tabitha.

"No thanks, I had a late lunch." She watched the chunks of spicy sirloin disappear within quick bites, then he wiped his mouth on the napkin. Seconds later, he snagged a couple of mini crab cakes. "I take it you missed a meal again today."

He munched. "No time…I had back-to-back meetings."

The man had a committed work ethic in line with her own. Tabitha actually admired that about him. But that said… "You need to make time." His gaze met hers. "Well, you do."

"Why Miss Seils, is it that you care about my welfare—" a grin creased his mouth as he chewed while bringing his thumb and index finger a scant space apart "—just a little?"

Tabitha couldn't contain her smirk. His looked so adorably sexy. "I thought this was supposed to be a business networking event. You didn't say anything about gambling." They accepted glasses of Chardonnay, and she stayed in step beside him.

"It's both. It's how this part of the world does business."

They couldn't walk two steps without someone stopping them to chat up Dominic.

"Aren't you popular. Is there anyone here you don't—" She tilted her head to see the blonde standing behind Dominic give him a tap on the shoulder. He turned and was met with a kiss on the cheek. Tabitha found herself being led forward once again by his hand on the small of her back. After a quick introduction and small talk, the woman, Julia, went on her way.

"You're in hot demand tonight," she muttered as they came up to a stocky bald man seated at a blackjack table.

"Evening, Federico. Glad you were able to make it." They shook hands.

"Dominic, good to see you. I postponed my departure until the morning and decided to take you up on your invitation," he said in a thick Spanish drawl. With a jack of hearts and a five of diamonds displayed, Federico scraped a finger across the table, signaling the dealer. "Hit me." A ten of spades flipped faceup. "Shit," he hissed, shaking his head. "It would seem Lady Luck isn't on my side tonight." He reared back to see around Dominic, his attention narrowing in on Tabitha. A smile filled out his flushed, pudgy cheeks. "On second thought—Good evening, madam. To whom do I owe the pleasure?"

"This is Tabitha Seils, one of the three partners of Chase Confections I told you about." Dominic turned to her. "Federico Cervantes owns a fleet of cruise liners abroad. My family's company designs and builds his ships."

"That they do." Federico came to his feet, and they moved away from the table. "Balaska Imperial and I have been doing business for years. It's a pleasure to meet you, Ms. Seils."

"Tabitha." She smiled. "You as well, Mr. Cervantes."

"Please call me Federico. Dominic says I'd be smart to have your desserts served aboard my boats. Tell me, what's the largest order your company has produced? Just one of my liners would require an order size of about ten thousand. Multiply that by seven. Can your company handle the volume?"

Wow! Tabitha took a gulp of her wine, practically emptying the glass to wet her suddenly parched tongue. The largest they'd catered was about five thousand. Once again, she cursed her business partners. Marketing was so not her forte.

She started in, talking about the company's history, her partners, the desserts Chase offered, even their most popular menu items, basically rambling. Nothing she said indicated Chase could handle an order of his magnitude. "Chase Confections is more than capable of meeting your needs, Federico." She tried to keep her features from betraying the long line of BS she'd just spewed. His dry expression said he wasn't impressed. Dominic took her glass and set it with his on a nearby table, then his hand clasped hers. He gave her a light squeeze as he directed his attention to the shipping magnate.

"Federico, here's a chance to work with one of the best pastry chefs in the country. Her desserts are like nothing you've ever tasted. I wouldn't steer you wrong."

Federico's gaze dipped to their linked hands, then shifted between them. "I see." He nodded. "You support your lady, of course. As you should."

"We're not—" Tabitha started but strong fingers tightened across her knuckles just enough to signal *shut up*.

"Indeed, I support everything she does, simply because she's a wonderful, amazing woman. To add to that, Tabitha's pastry skills are top-notch." Dominic stared at the other man. Bold. Unwavering.

Federico smiled. "Well, Tabitha—" his attention moved to her "—I trust Dominic. His confidence in you is good enough for me. It's a verbal yes. I'll have my attorney contact you. If he says the numbers are favorable, I'll sign."

"That'll work." Dominic grinned and shook Federico's hand.

Tabitha followed suit, in complete admiration for the ease with which Dominic maneuvered, manipulated, and ultimately conquered. But what awed her the most was his kind words about her.

Holy crap! A seventy-thousand-count repeat order. She couldn't wait to tell Kennedi and Evie.

"Now that business is out of the way, let us play. Perhaps, Tabitha, you will be my good luck charm."

She took Federico's proffered arm.

"You two go ahead. I'm going to grab something to eat at the bar."

The soft, warm, lingering kiss Dominic pressed on her mouth stunned her. He reared back, his gaze delving into hers. Those beautiful blue eyes smoldered bright and hot before he gave a slight wink. "I'll see you in a few, sweetheart." Another quick peck, then he strode off.

"Shall we?" Federico grinned and folded his hand over hers at the bend of his arm.

It was an act. Dominic had been pretending for Federico's benefit. But wow, that kiss warmed Tabitha all the way down to her toes. She licked her lips in search of any remnants of his taste.

Sleeping together did not affirm a relationship. She recognized the sudden tightness in her chest for what it was: disappointment riding alongside regret that she'd rejected his interest in her during their first meeting many months ago. She cursed herself for not seeing what had been right in front of her then and for not recognizing what Evie had so easily seen.

A little more than a half hour later, having watched Federico blow thousands of dollars on fruitless table sport, Tabitha left him in search of Dominic. She narrowed in on him seated on a barstool among the crowded bodies lining the L-shaped, rich mahogany wood surface. A smile creased his lips as he spoke to the woman leaning against the bar beside him. She tipped her head to one side, a seductive sort of head roll. Waves upon waves of dark hair flowed over one creamy tanned shoulder. Dominic's stare dipped only briefly to the woman's low-cut black dress before he took a hefty bite of his burger. The man's muscle-cut body was in stark contrast to the amount of food he seemed to consume.

Tabitha watched as the woman leaned closer and whispered something in his ear. A grin curved his mouth as he chewed. She walked up behind them. "Dominic?"

He quickly brought up a napkin and wiped his mouth, then swiveled, facing her. A grin heightened his handsome features. "Hey, you."

Tabitha looked at the woman, meeting her eye to eye. She was even more stunning up close. Lustrous gray irises the hue of slick metal. Pearl-pink tinted full lips. Perfect tan—didn't matter if it was bottled or sun-gifted, it was flawless. She had an easy, natural sophistication about her.

"You get enough to eat?" Tabitha asked him. His arm

hooked at her waist; a hand rested comfortably on her hip.

"Yes. Sweetheart, this is Christina Kaye. Christina, meet my lady, Tabitha Seils."

His lady? He was apparently still in character. She looked at the woman again and noticed the leggy brunette's expression had momentarily gone rigid as she latched on to Tabitha's extended hand. "Nice to meet you."

"You too." Christina's stare moved to Dominic. "You and I together would be unstoppable." She gave another glance Tabitha's way. "But you've made your point. Quite clear, I would say." She smiled at him rather weakly. "You all enjoy your night."

As Christina disappeared into the crowd, Dominic's arm cinched a bit tighter. "I can explain. She's a—"

Tabitha pressed her fingertips to his lips. She wasn't interested in getting the four-one-one on any of his past dalliances. Instead, she centered her inquisitiveness on continuing to get to know the man who'd been so generously sweet and wonderfully attentive to her these past days.

"I appreciate what you did back there with Federico, helping Chase land a major contract tonight." She leaned against his powerful build, soaking up the support of his strong embrace, and straightened his bow tie. "I'd like to show you just how much, Mr. Balaska."

His focus lifted from his study of the exposed swells of her breasts and met her gaze with a crooked grin. "I don't know, Miss Seils. Wouldn't that be breaking rules of professional etiquette? Mixing business with pleasure?"

She liked that he teased her, and came in at his ear, whispering, "Though mixing business with pleasure can result in very nasty and dirty consequences, Mr. Balaska, it can also bloom some very satisfying rewards."

"Hmm." His brow rose. With his hands anchored on her hips, he glanced around before bringing her between the split of his legs, their lips nearly touching. "So, what's it going to be? Nasty and dirty, or very satisfying?" His tone was a sexy, smooth register that reverberated and warmed every nerve ending.

"Well, judging by what I've seen of you so far—" she palmed and squeeze his rock-hard thighs "—I'd say all three."

Smiling, she took his hand and led the way through the crowd. Federico, with a man beside him, called out to Dominic. The other man signaled with an energetic wave.

"Keep going," Dominic urged her, but Tabitha slowed.

"We can't, unless you want to risk the deal we made with Federico. You go say hi. I'll head up." She gave a light tug of his chin, delivering a touch of her lips to his. "You want to keep in good standing with him."

"What I want is us in a hot shower and you in my bed. I'll be up in ten." His lust unapologetically glowed in his hot gaze.

Ripe with anticipation, picturing him wet and naked, she hurried through the lobby, rode the elevator up, and entered the suite. She waited ten minutes, which turned into twenty. By the half-hour mark, she got in the shower but took her time, expecting he'd come through the door at any second and join her. When she could no longer stand the feel of her pruney fingers, she dried off and sat on the edge of her bed, coating her warm skin in scented moisturizer.

With the shades up and the lamp at a soft glow, she slid in between the sheets. Her eyelids shuttered almost instantly.

The cool hand sliding along her thigh pulled her awake. Dominic's crisp, clean scent from a recent shower enveloped her. She squinted at the clock—almost two hours had slipped by.

"So much for ten minutes," she murmured sleepily and leaned her head back on his shoulder, reviving beneath his kiss as he rubbed his nude body against hers under the comfy bedding.

"Federico's friend wouldn't shut up," he whispered against her lips. "I expected to find you in my bed."

"Does it matter?" She rolled over and slipped her fingers into his damp hair. He began kissing his way down the column of her neck to the arching offer of her breasts.

"Not even a little bit." His tongue flicked, circled, and teased her nipple, working it into a stiff, achy knot. He skated light kisses across her stomach and along the curves of her hips as he settled his wide shoulders between her thighs. His mouth pressed against her clit, his tongue licking unhurriedly.

She snaked her fingers in his hair for purchase as he took his time tasting her for long glorious minutes as she panted his name over and over. Then, he trailed gentle kisses up her body, circling her left nipple with his tongue, licking along her collarbone, snaking kisses around her throat and up to claim her mouth.

When he entered her, moving with deep, determined thrusts, she responded with just as much neediness, driving their scorching, undulating limbs to a splintery climax. He buried his face at the crook of her neck. She wrapped her arms around his broad back, relishing in his heavy breathing at her ear, in his rapidly beating heart against her breasts, in the satiated weight of him, in every part of him.

"That woman tonight…"

He came up on his elbows, and Tabitha cracked opened an eye while stroking his smooth buttocks. "You're killing my orgasm buzz, Balaska. It's cool. I don't need to know the—"

Gentle, yet firm fingertips covered her mouth before he pressed his lips to hers then rolled off her onto his side.

"Christina Kaye is a VC—venture capitalist."

"I'm aware of what it is."

"I met her some months ago at an event one attends when looking for investment funding. I turned down her offer because she was expecting more than an interest in my project. Are you familiar with what went down with Trent and his ex-wife?"

"Kennedi filled me in." Trenton had met his ex in a very similar fashion. The woman ended up cheating on him.

"Well, then you understand the proposition Christina wanted to make with me. I witnessed firsthand what my brother experienced with his ex. I'm not about that shit. What you saw tonight was her trying to convince me why partnering with her would be advantageous. I told her I was seeing someone to shut down any idea she had of changing my mind. You happened to walk up at the perfect time, so I just went with it. I guess that's the long and short of it."

As desperate as he no doubt was—on the brink of losing his trust fund in six months and in need of investment money—he didn't take Christina's offer. A newfound trust bloomed as all her barriers fell away.

"So Christina wanted to trade sex for investment funding?"

"She's never come out and said it, but I know the code words. I'm not about that."

Tabitha arched an eyebrow. "That's to say, you're principled when it comes to sex."

He drew back. "Don't sound so shocked." He laughed, then his eyes held hers as the tips of his fingers traced a slow caress along the angle of her left collarbone, swirled the hollow of her throat and continued to the other. "I have standards," he said softly.

"What sort of standards?" She held his gaze while performing a thorough exploration of his rippled abdomen, playing in the fine tuft of dark chest hair, and stroking over his hard biceps. "What do you look for in a woman?"

"Well, she has to be intelligent, adventurous—maybe likes to rock climb, enjoys UFC, and makes a kickass blueberry scone." They shared grins. "She's not afraid to step out of the box, knows what she wants and goes after it."

"I'm planning to adopt a baby," she blurted. With her breath locked in her lungs, the familiar stark silence saturated the air as it inevitably did whenever she mentioned the A word.

"You're adopting a baby?" He stared.

"Yes."

He rolled out of bed and crossed to the bathroom. Her heart was hammering so hard, it felt as if it would plow clean through her breastbone by the time he emerged and slipped back beneath the covers.

"What baby? When?"

Her stomach flipped wildly. "It's through an adoption agency. I'm being considered along with two other couples for a baby that's due in about five months."

"Oh." His silence revived her apprehension. "What made you decide this, if you don't mind me asking?"

She took his hand and guided it along her tattoo that camouflaged the slightly raised scar. "Ovarian cancer. I had one of my ovaries removed." A pained looked washed over his features. She felt that same pain start to crawl its way from the shadows, but she shoved it back. "Though the other doesn't function normally, I got pregnant, but suffered a miscarriage early on. The likelihood it would happen again is slim to none. In other words, I can't have children."

He caressed her cheek with the backs of his fingers, his thumb delicately stroking. "I can't imagine what you went through, what you suffered."

"Yes." She swallowed hard to contain the remembered grief.

"Any child would be extremely fortunate to have you as a mother. If it's what you want, you should do it."

He didn't convey even a slight twitch of objection, no dissuading commentary. She tipped her head up and kissed him with trembling lips, working through the tightness in her throat. He turned off the light, then tucked her in close. She rested her head against his calmly beating heart, her arms curling around him.

"Good night, beautiful."

Soft lips tenderly pressed against her brow, and she released a long sigh, feeling an incredible swell of contentment. "Good night."

HIS PHONE BUZZING in his pants pocket on the floor pulled Dominic from a comatose-like slumber. He reached over the side of the bed, tapped off the annoyance, then rolled to find Tabitha's sleeping and beautifully naked form bathed in the beginning touches of dawn.

She lay stretched out on her stomach, facing him. His heart did a kind of pitter-patter—wild, frizzy hair draped across smooth skin and soft curves he was now quite familiar with. His gaze swept over her in a hot, greedy probe. Long legs and the tauntingly sweet contour of her ass begged to be kissed. His well-used dick throbbed and bobbed against his stomach, wanting inside her again.

Her eyes fluttered open, peeking through the voluminous strands of hair that partially covered her face. That unusual quiver came into his chest once more. "Hey, you." He brushed back long tresses and liked how the morning daybreak caught in the hazel jewels of her eyes.

"Morning," she said, her soft, sleepy voice a pleasing timbre. "Did I wake you? Kennedi claims I sometimes snore."

"It was like sleeping next to a railway station." Her eyes widened, and he laughed. "Just kidding."

She grinned and delivered a playful slap to his chest. "You're not funny."

"You weren't snoring. Not at all." He tucked copious

locks behind her ear.

"Thanks for last night…er…" She gave a small smile. "I mean helping Chase possibly land that huge contract." She rolled onto her back and half bent a lean leg upward, an arm lazily draped above her head.

Dominic's gaze greedily soaked up the sight. "No need to thank me." He followed her stare down to his rapidly rising erection stretching rigidly along his stomach.

Her eyes met his. "I probably should get in the shower and head to work. It's my last day at Pearl," she said, yet her fingers curled around his cock, her smooth, determined palm leisurely stroking.

"Yes, it's your last day." He rolled on top of her and parted her legs with his knees. "They wanted us to get along. I think we succeeded at that, wouldn't you say?" he asked as he eased inside the tightness of her. He wanted to go slow, savor every second, but the vigor of her rocking hips didn't permit him leisurely and gentle.

She smiled. "Without a doubt." While he had her writhing and moaning beneath him with her nails raking his back to his ass, his cell phone on the nightstand rang. Ignoring the disruption, he coaxed her onto her stomach, settled in between her legs, and entered her sex from behind, once again finding her sweet spot. With their rhythm back on track, he fingered her clit, stroking the swollen nub in time to his swiftly working hips. The phone stopped ringing, then started again.

"Someone really wants to get ahold of you," she breathed out. "Maybe you should answer."

"No." He latched on to a breast and nipped the back of

her neck, pinning her in place as he pumped in and out of her with ferocious speed.

"Dominic, answer it."

He rolled off her and snatched the device. Chest heaving, he let out a low curse and opened the line. "Mom, it's five forty-five in the morning here. I'm sleeping." Tabitha silently mouthed *liar* and planted a light kiss on the center of his chest. "I'll call you later."

"You said that two days ago. We must discuss the trust documents. The attorney sent over the notification reminder of the clauses that must be satisfied. Time is running out, son. I don't understand why you cannot see the urgency."

Dominic hissed low as he watched Tabitha take his dick between her soft lips and circle her sweet tongue around the head before sucking the tip. She looked up at him, wearing a wicked grin before slowly sinking his length to the far reaches of her throat.

"Dominic Savino, are you listening to me?"

"Ye-yes. I'm listening. I do see the urgency. Mom, I promise, I'll call later to discuss it." He lightly fisted Tabitha's hair and ground his molars to combat the pressure building in his balls. "I have to go."

"All right. I will expect your call. Good-bye."

"Bye." He disconnected. "You're bad—you know that?"

Tabitha popped him free from her gloriously warm mouth and came up over him. "I see you have one of them too." She guided his shaft back into her slick channel.

"One of what?" He gripped her hip, setting their rhythm.

"A loving mother who forgets you're an adult." She waved a hand. "Same here." Then she planted her palms on his chest and rode him with quick lifts and deep grinds.

Dominic flipped her onto her back and slowed the pace, wanting to enjoy her. She released a low moan of encouragement as her hands went into his hair, prowled his shoulders, and slid down his back to his ass, squeezing.

Their tongues mated sweetly as their rocking motion built a persistent momentum. The feel of her so tight and wet and warm, the intermittent pulsating of her inner walls… He latched on to the wild tide of pleasure but pulled out not a second too soon, taking his release between their fevered bodies.

When he finally rolled onto his back, they lay quietly staring up at the neon lights pouring in through the windows, streaking across the ceiling.

"I couldn't help hearing your phone conversation. Your mother's still on you about your trust."

He turned his head and met her fixed gaze. "Pretty much."

She exhaled deeply. "I assume we're talking about a large sum. Otherwise, she wouldn't be pressing you."

"Twenty mil, depending on the market. Another sixty if I produce an offspring within the first year. I'm only interested in the twenty. It'll cover what I need."

Her eyes widened then settled, regarding him. "I see." She climbed out of bed and left the bedroom. He could hear the sound of the shower.

Shit. He regretted saying anything to her about the damn trust. He hitched a low breath when she appeared in the doorway mere seconds later, wearing a towel, looking like a sculpted goddess.

"I'll do it."

"Do what?"

"I'll help you satisfy your trust."

Dominic's eyelids fluttered. "You'll help me?" He couldn't believe his ears.

"Yes. It'll be temporary, of course. They do quick weddings here, right?"

Stunned, he simply stared, bowled over for a moment. "You're sure?"

With arms crossed, she leaned a shoulder against the doorframe, confidence apparent, certain…the fierce woman he knew her to be. "I wouldn't have offered if I wasn't sure. I'm going to go take a shower. Let me know what you decide." She pivoted.

"Yes!" He leaped from the bed and caught her hand. "I do." The double entendre left them both staring. "What I'm trying to say is, thank you for what you're offering to do for me."

"I'm helping a friend. We're friends, right?" A soft smile highlighted her beautiful face.

"Most definitely." He'd like to think they were dipping their toes into more than that, but he wouldn't force his way in where she might not want to go with him.

"Tell me more about this trust."

"I haven't actually read it. But according to my mother, it's been in the family as far back as my great-great-grandfather. I have my mother's name, Balaska, instead of my father's, which was Volante. Each heir and heiress must take the family name tied to the trust. As I explained, the women must marry by age twenty-five and the men by age thirty-one in order to exercise the funds due him or her. For the heiress, it's written that her name, not her husband's, must be carried down to her firstborn or her inheritance will be forfeited back to the trust."

"So the trust belongs to your mother's family?"

"Yes. It's a ridiculous clause, but no one has ever protested it. As for you and me making things legal, so to speak, it's pretty simple, really. We have to provide a license to prove we're married. Once the attorneys validate it, they'll notify the executor to release the funds. So, how does fifty K sound?"

"What do you mean?"

"I want to compensate you for helping me."

"Oh, then it sounds like a joke. One hundred thousand. I have adoption fees to cover…and there might be unforeseen incidentals."

That erased any question he had on where things stood. Line effectively drawn. The fact that she wasn't out for a big payday—and instead her nominal monetary objective centered around her desire to adopt, it should have brought him comfort. Yet he only felt upset. "That'll work."

She cupped his face in her hands and her mouth covered his. He surrendered to the sweet demand of her tongue for a heart-stopping moment, then broke away before she was ready.

Because he was a bit wounded, he drew on his all-business strength. "I'll take care of the license, and we'll go tonight."

Chapter Thirteen

"I'M ALL PACKED," Tabitha called to Dominic from her room.

"You're sure? Because you said that ten minutes ago."

She rolled her luggage into the living room to find him seated on the couch, scrolling through his phone. She smirked. "See?"

He came to his feet. The man could work the hell out of a designer suit. But now, dressed as he was in a simple pullover shirt and well-fitted dark denims, he easily got a rise out of her.

She checked her watch. Tossing the thought of giving that amazing appendage of his one last ride for the road, she walked her horny behind to the entryway. They'd spent a good two hours that morning rumpling the sheets.

"It's a private jet. Won't the pilot wait for me to arrive? And when do you return to D.C.?" She'd taken him up on his offer to fly back on the company plane and looked forward to the impending quiet…and extra legroom.

"The pilot can always adjust the departure time, yes. But it's easier to simply stay on schedule," he told her as he took her luggage. "I'm here another week." He pulled opened the door. "After you, Miss Seils…well, you're Balaska now." He adjusted the diamond bracelet circling her wrist he'd given her, a small sealing of their union.

"We should keep that to ourselves for now." He delivered a long, hot, greedy kiss. Breathless, she took a small step away to curb the tempting desire to drag him back inside and have her way with him.

"I have a lot to catch up on when I return home. The store as well as the construction. The interior furniture and fixtures are next on my list to tackle. Not to mention, Evie sent me a list of three new custom orders received just yesterday. I also have a new intern who's starting soon."

"And the adoption. You have that going."

"Yes, that too. I received an email the other day. There are some additional papers I still need to provide the agency." Her head angled. She frowned. "What's that for?"

"What's what?"

"That look. You made a face."

"I didn't."

"Your face does this thing. I've seen it enough at the construction site and even at Dabney's, when you don't approve or agree with something I've said."

He sighed. "It strikes me as curious. Why isn't the adoption on your to-do list?"

"It was…is."

"Not until I put it there. You're up before dawn working at your bakery every day on top of managing the construction on the new place and all the other things you mentioned. You said yourself you haven't completed needed paperwork for the adoption. If it's a top priority…"

Tabitha's eyes narrowed, and he brought up a hand.

"All I'm saying is you have a lot going on. A child isn't going to want to take a fourth or fifth seat."

Kennedi, Evie, her family, and now him. "I see you were just humoring me when you said I'd be a great mother."

"You *will* be a terrific mother…when you've set your life to be one."

His words struck as sharp and precisely as any knife would have. "You've satisfied your trust agreement, so now you can share how you really perceive me. Maybe it was your plan all along. I was your target. This entire week was you manipulating, working to get me to…" She glanced at the double roll of perfect diamonds circling her wrist and what it symbolized to her as the wool he'd pulled over her eyes was now lifted. For so long she'd sat alone in darkness, afraid to feel, afraid to trust. But the glimmer that found its way back into her heart, he'd been the cause, and she'd chanced it in his care, only for him to snuff it out like a traitorous thief. She'd been here before. Her brow knitted from the shocking familiar pain his cruel betrayal would leave in her soul.

She stared into the eyes that held the blade as a choke of emotions knotted in her throat. Swallowing hard, she snatched her luggage from him and crossed to the elevator, delivering a hard push of the button. Thankfully, the doors parted almost immediately, allowing her to hold on to a small scrap of dignity.

When he started to follow her inside, she brought up a hand. "Don't. I wouldn't want you to accuse me of…who the hell knows what else."

"You're getting it all wrong, Tabitha."

"No, I think I have it just right." She shoved away his hand that held the door open and let it shut him out.

Chapter Fourteen

DOMINIC ENTERED CHASE Confections and approached Evie behind the counter.

"Dom, hi."

"Good evening, Evie."

They moved off to the side to get out of Amy's way, attending to a customer.

Just then, Kennedi exited through the swing door.

"Dom, I thought you weren't due back until Friday."

"Change of plans. Is Tabitha in?"

"What's going on between you two? Tabitha told Evie and me never to speak your name in front of her. Her regard for you is worse than before she left. What the heck happened?"

Dominic winced. "We had a misunderstanding. I came here to try to straighten things out."

Kennedi arched an eyebrow. "You changed your entire work schedule and flew back home for the sole purpose of making amends with Tabitha?"

It sounded pretty crazy out loud. Theirs was a marriage of convenience. Yet it felt as though he'd committed a form of betrayal against his partner.

"That's really sweet, Dom," Evie crooned.

"I'm doubting your friend will share that sentiment."

"It's that bad, huh?"

"I'm afraid so."

"You're here to make peace with her. That's good." Kennedi gestured with a thumb over her shoulder. "You know where to find her."

He made his way to the kitchen. The evening calm was a stark contrast to the hectic afternoon activity the last time he'd been in the rear of the store.

She stood with her back to him, washing her hands at the sink. A mere forty-eight hours ago, he'd filled his palms with her raven locks as he claimed her soft lips and made her moan, writhe, and grind beneath the weight of his body. Now she likely loathed the very ground where he stood. For him, the desire to touch her, hold her, simmered like a sudden heat wave, but he knew to tread carefully.

"Tabitha?" Once again, he witnessed the tension straighten her spine as tight as a trapeze wire. Her head whipped around. Her expression made the hairs on the back of his neck stand up. If looks could kill, he'd already have his guts spattered across the tiled floor.

"Balaska, shouldn't you be in Vegas spreading your charm to some unsuspecting soul right about now?" Her eyes followed his to the bracelet glinting at her wrist, then her glare locked on him across the metal table. "I have work to do. Those pesky priorities." She sneered while grabbing a knife from the line of sharp cutlery magnetized on the wall. She moved to the center prep table where a large sheet cake lay unfrosted and began carving around the edges. "Bridget," she called, and the young apprentice snapped forward. With an easy dismissal of Dominic, she started in on the how-tos.

"I flew back to talk to you. Can we go somewhere private?"

"You should've saved the jet fuel. I'm busy." She hadn't bothered turning around and hardly skipped a beat in her instructions.

He walked up beside her. "Tabitha, I'd like us to talk."

"Not necessary. You made yourself very clear." She moved with Bridget to a shelf lined with baking products.

"I feel I didn't." Dominic looked at Bridget, who offered an awkward smile, then around the orderly kitchen and at the young man loading dishes in the washer, the only other staff member in the room. "Okay, if you won't speak with me in private, I'll stand here and talk. I didn't marry yo—"

"Everybody out!" Tabitha swung around. "Ronny?" The young man jumped at the sound of her alert and turned off the water. Bridget had already skirted out like someone had yelled fire. "Please, go out front."

When it was just the two of them, she marched forward and, per her habit, he assumed he was meant to follow her as she stalked into the small office at the rear and then closed the door behind him.

What was the purpose of clearing out the kitchen if they were going to have it out behind closed doors? He wouldn't dare ask. No knives present gave him a small reassurance he'd get to walk out in one piece.

With a long sigh, she scrubbed her fingers at her brow. "Let me make something clear, Balaska. I'm not upset with you. Sleeping with you and the whole marriage arrangement, those mistakes are on me. I'm pissed at myself for that."

"It wasn't a mistake, at least not for me. What we shared meant something." She let go a dry chuckle. "I didn't use you. What I was trying to say was…you take on so much. Having a kid would mean making some major adjustments, maybe even letting go of some of the things you're doing. And, quite honestly, I found it odd that you didn't have the adoption matter at the forefront."

"Thanks for the wisdom." She snorted and pivoted toward the door.

He caught her hand but quickly let go when she turned and aimed her hot glare his way. "Look, I meant what I said. I do feel you'll be a terrific mom. And as for me playing you, I've had plenty of opportunities to get married."

"Oh, I'm very much aware. There's Valerie and Celeste. Let us not forget Miranda and who knows how many others."

He didn't take the bait. "What I'm saying is, the idea of getting hitched to someone I don't care about, don't have feelings for, isn't something I was eager to do. Which is why I was within six months of forfeiting my trust."

"So you're saying asking me to marry you simply to settle your trust was never a motive you considered?"

His hesitation brought a scowl to her features. "I thought about it, yes, but—"

"But I offered and fell right into your plan."

"Yes…no." Shit, he was fucking things up even more. And it was too soon. Evidently, forty-eight hours hadn't been enough time for her to cool. "I nixed the idea long before we became intimately involved."

"This is…is…" She shook her head. "Wow. I don't

know which insults me the most. The fact that you take me for a fool or your lack of sincerity about my plans to adopt." She nodded. "Yep, the marriage, sleeping with you, all of it—that foolhardiness is completely on me."

She took hold of the doorknob, then gave a look over her shoulder. "I'm a woman of my word. I'll keep our arrangement on paper. As for you and me, that's finished."

Expressionless, she pulled open the door, moved to the swing door, and held it open wide with her back pressed against it.

"Good evening, Mr. Balaska."

The door swung heavily, nearly catching him in the back on his way out.

Chapter Fifteen

Tabitha carried three filled glasses of pinot into the living room. She handed one to Kennedi lounging on the couch and another to Evie seated on the floor who had Dixie in her lap and Percy at her side. Taking a sip, Tabitha curled up in the armchair, tucking her legs under her.

"I have to say, I'm a bit surprised Dominic would do such a thing," Kennedi remarked.

Tabitha had brought her girlfriends up to speed on what took place in Vegas just before she departed, but with one exception. She gave a glance at her tennis bracelet that bonded her to Dominic like any ring would, and was part of the story she hadn't shared with her friends.

"Twenty million is quite a lot to lose," Evie said and took a swallow of her wine. "If Dominic tried to manipulate you to help him get his trust fund, that wasn't cool. That said, you have to know we support you wanting to adopt. Sorry if we came off to the contrary."

"Yes, we were taken by surprise. That's all." Kennedi got up and enveloped Tabitha's shoulders in a warm embrace, then returned to the couch. "We have your back."

"That's right, sista girl, we got you." Evie raised her glass before taking another sip. "We're your built-in babysitters.

That's what I told the lady from the adoption agency who interviewed me last week."

Tabitha's heart overflowed with love; having their support meant everything. "As for Dominic, there is no if. He set out to use me."

"He probably feels desperate. Six months is not a lot of time," Evie returned. Her head angled. "I don't know, Tab. Would it be so bad? I mean, you two would only have to stay married long enough that he'd get his trust, then get the marriage annulled. The bonus—you could indulge in the fact that you're married, be it temporary, and enjoy the perks that come with it."

Tabitha and Kennedi stared at Evie as she sat there stroking the rabbits. "By perks, you mean sex?" Kennedi asked.

"That's exactly what I mean. I see nothing wrong with it. Life's too short. And look at him. He's hot. Not a bad trade-off, if you ask me."

Tabitha gaped at her friend. The separation from her husband, Patrick, seemed to have freed more than Evie's self-worth. "Dominic and I got married and we slept together in Vegas," she said and held up her arm, displaying the bracelet that hadn't left her wrist from the moment he put it there.

Wine sprayed from Kennedi's mouth. She jumped to her feet. Evie choked on her mouthful, coughing.

Tabitha grabbed the box of tissues from the side table and tossed several to the both of them.

"You and Dominic got married?" Kennedi's eyes were wide as saucers as she sprinted the short distance and examined the bracelet. "When I said get to know him, I didn't mean marry the man."

"Oh my God!" Evie joined her. "Now it all makes sense." A slow smile curved her lips. She smacked her thigh, startling Dixie in the crook of her arm. "I was right again about you two. I knew it."

"It also explains why he came back on Sunday instead of on Friday as planned," Kennedi said.

"That's right." Evie nodded. "He flew home to smooth things over with his wife." She grinned.

Tabitha sipped from her glass and looked on as the two worked their case. "We're married on paper only. Once he gets his trust fund, we'll get an annulment."

"Yeah, yeah. Details. Spill the tea, and I mean the whole damn cup." Evie sat Dixie on the floor and bent to her knees.

"What she said." Kennedi inched forward in her seat, clearly prepping for a juicy account.

Often, Tabitha thought about how terrific her time spent with Dominic had been. But it wasn't real. What bloomed between them happened in Vegas, where it would stay. "There's nothing to tell. We both understand that the marriage is temporary. As for the two of us, that's over."

Their eager stares flattened.

"Tab, hear me out." Evie sat back on her shins. "Is there a small possibility you might have misunderstood Dominic?" She held a cautious stare. "From what you told us, he merely said what Kennedi and I've said to you." Evie looked at Kennedi who gave a subtle, tentative nod. "I mean, you have a lot going on. Managing the kitchen and the new store's construction."

"Don't forget the interns," Kennedi said. "You do a great

job with them. Carlos will tell anyone who asks that he wouldn't have graduated culinary school if not for interning under your tutelage. And I could tell that Bridget and Ronny couldn't wait for you to get back from Vegas. I tried to step into your role while you were away but didn't come close to filling your shoes."

"The point is, we know you love doing all that you do and wonder…worry if you'll be able to let go of some of it to devote to a baby right now," Evie supplemented.

"By no means is this to say we don't support you in whatever you wish to do," Kennedi tagged on. "That said, maybe you used the situation with the adoption to push Dominic away. You went through hell with Jeff. I understand it's hard to start down that road after what you suffered."

Tabitha scooped Percy from the floor and stroked his soft pelt while sipping her wine. What if they were right? To let Dominic in, she'd be forced to confront her feelings with unguarded eyes. But she was afraid of her emotions, afraid to offer that space in her heart to him…

And afraid not to.

STRETCHED OUT ON the couch, Dominic reached above his head to the side table for his ringing cell. He opened the line to his brother. "What's up?"

"You tell me. What the fuck is wrong with you? I specifically told you not to involve Tabitha in your stupid scheme, but you did it anyway."

Dominic sat up. "I didn't. There was no scheme." He jerked the phone away from his ear to escape his brother's booming voice.

"The hell there wasn't! Kennedi told me you and Tabitha got married in Vegas, so don't fucking lie to me! Now she's not speaking to you. Go figure."

"We had a misunderstanding. Tabitha thought—" Dominic began.

"Misunderstanding, my ass! You accomplished exactly what you set out to do. Kennedi asked if I was aware of what you were planning. Since I don't intend to ever lie to my future wife, she wasn't happy with the answer. I knew this shit would happen."

"Dude, listen. I—"

"No, you listen. Don't bother showing up for the dinner Mom's throwing for Kennedi and me. In other words, stay out of my sight."

The line went dead. Dominic flung the phone across the couch.

Fuck.

Chapter Sixteen

"HEY, YOU DROPPED your sweater. I'd pick it up, but it's becoming more and more difficult these days."

Tabitha looked up from her iPad at the smiling pregnant, blonde woman stroking her extended belly. "Oh, thanks."

"You won't be needing it this afternoon. It's supposed to hit eighty degrees."

"Sharon, here you go."

Tabitha knew that voice. Her head whipped sharply, her breath catching. The sight of her ex, Jeffrey, exiting the Starbucks trapped the air tight in her chest. His even stride came to a halt, their eyes locking. When had he crossed her path into the store? His intense stare faltered a moment before he continued to the table and handed the woman, *Sharon*, a drink. Sharon slipped an arm around his waist.

Eyes fluttering from shock, Tabitha swallowed hard to get her lips to move. Her stare zeroed in again on the roundness of the woman's pregnant belly.

"Tabitha, how have you been?"

"I'm, uh, good." Aside from the neatly groomed goatee that added definition to the weak angle of his chin and jawbone structure, he still looked the same—chestnut-brown eyes, flushed cheeks, clean-shaven crown. Not unattractive, but he wouldn't be considered handsome in the traditional sense either.

"You two know each other?" Sharon looked between them.

Tabitha's attention moved to the smiling woman, then back at Jeff.

"Sharon, this is Tabitha, a, uh, friend of mine," he said, finally finding his manners.

Friend! We were engaged to be married, you prick! Keeping her cool, she said, "Nice to meet you."

"You too."

"You're pregnant." The words unceremoniously fell out of Tabitha's mouth as she continued to gawk at the woman's stomach while her own turned over and over.

"Seven months along," Sharon answered happily, continuing a circular caress with both hands atop her baby mound.

The diamond on her finger caught the sun's rays. The stone was easily twice the size of the one he'd given Tabitha. Shock, anger, hurt—each battled for dominance within the center of her chest.

She watched as Jeffrey brought up that hand and kissed it. "Nice ring. You're married?" she asked.

"Engaged." Sharon beamed. "The date is set for next month on the twentieth."

"We're keeping it small, just family and a few friends," Jeffrey said.

Tabitha swallowed rapidly to keep the lemon poppy-seed muffin mixed with the coffee churning in her gut from rising back up. Jeffrey was engaged and he and Sharon were going to have a baby.

He'd told her he wasn't ready to have children. When she found out she was pregnant, he'd felt she'd deceived him about being unable to conceive. She hadn't lied. His ass cheated to get out of marrying her, and here he stood happily ready to go the distance with this woman. The audacity! Tabitha's foot itched to kick him in the balls.

"How long have you two been together? Specifically, when did you two meet?" She held her stare on Jeffrey. Oh, he understood her meaning, all right.

"Let me see if he remembers the date we met," Sharon said with a smirk. "Go on, tell her."

"It'll be a year next Wednesday," Jeffrey answered, his voice wobbling.

"Wrong, but you're close. Next Friday will be one year." Sharon laughed, shaking her head. "Men. If it's not related to sports, their brains can't hold the information." She grasped his chin and pulled him in for a peck on the lips. "But I'll keep him anyway." She and Jeffrey chuckled.

Tabitha pictured herself performing a Moe Howard move—Stooge-slap those wide, jolly grins off their faces. Well, not Sharon necessarily, since she'd just confirmed she hadn't been a party to Jeffrey's treachery. But he definitely deserved a good punch in the nose...and a nice hard kick to his jewels.

This hurts. This really fucking hurts. Dropping her eyes from the happy couple, she took a sip of her coffee to try to keep control of her emotions, mask the sting.

"We're on our way to pick out baby furniture," Sharon

remarked. She elbowed Jeffrey playfully. "This one's more excited about the task than I am."

"Uh, how's the bakery? I saw the commercial. It's relocating, right?" Jeffrey draped an arm around his fiancée's shoulder.

"Yes. It's doing good." Done with the awkward and forced small talk, she gestured at her iPad. "Thought I'd get some reading in."

He nodded. "I guess it's just you, your iPad, and your coffee."

His smirk was mocking, and his words twisted that horrible place in her memory. Her eyes flashed to his. "It's not a crime, is it?"

"Ah, now that's the Tabby I remember." With fingers perched like cat claws, he added, "Watch out, she might strike." Jeffrey playfully did a duck-and-dodge step. "I'm only teasing."

The double-chirp of a car's lock made all of them turn their heads. Tabitha's eyes widened at the sight of Dominic making his way across the cobbled sidewalk. He came up to the table.

"Good morning," he said cheerfully before his hand went to the back of her neck. Fingers caressed her nape as he leaned down and kissed her mouth deeply, giving her a thorough tonguing while moaning a little. She stiffened then relaxed into his kiss, a hot, lovers' kiss, sucking it in like new air. He drew back and gave a subtle wink.

"Sorry I'm late. Were you waiting long?" he asked.

It was as though the heavens opened up and the angel, Dominic Balaska, dropped down at her side, leaving Jeffrey gawking.

"Sweetheart, aren't you going to introduce us?" Dominic asked, smiling at the couple who stared back at him, catatonic.

Sweetheart. That pulled Tabitha out of her trance. She could play along. "Uh, Dominic, this is Jeffrey, my ex-fiancé, and his fiancée, Sharon."

Sharon gasped and jerked her head to Jeff. "Ex-fiancée! She's your *ex*-fiancée? You never mentioned you were engaged before."

Jeffrey blinked rapidly, looking as though he was searching for words.

"Jeffrey!" Sharon yelled with palms on her generous hips.

"Well, I-I—"

"Sharon, it's a pleasure to meet you. Please call me Dom." He shook her hand, then extended it to Jeffrey. "So you're *the* Jeffrey. It's a pleasure to shake your hand. I'm really glad we finally get to meet. You know, put a face with a name." Dominic wore a cool grin.

A look of pain briefly washed over Jeffrey's face as the men locked palms. Dominic delivered a brawny, knuckle-crunching grip, shake, and release that left the man subtly flexing the bones and rubbing away the sting against the side of his jeans.

What was Dominic up to? He knew nothing about her and her ex. And in between scowling at Jeff, Sharon was practically drooling over Dominic. The poor woman giggled and snorted like a crushing schoolgirl, melting right where she stood. Who could blame her? Tabitha had to admit Dominic looked smoking hot casually dressed in medium blue denims, a pale blue, short-sleeved Ralph Lauren polo shirt that fitted his upper physique to a tee, and black leather loafers. A pair of smoked-lens aviators sat perched atop his dark, wavy locks.

"Jeff, my man, no disrespect intended to your lovely fiancée, Sharon, here. I simply couldn't fathom why someone would let this remarkable woman get away." Dominic brushed the backs of his fingers lightly along Tabitha's cheek. "I tell you it baffles me. But lucky for me you did." Dominic chuckled deep.

"I…uh—" Jeffrey started.

"Every morning when I wake up to this stunningly beautiful face, I say to myself, her ex, Jeff, must be a damn fool to let such a rare, precious gem slip through his fingers."

Tabitha's eyes flashed up, and Dominic grinned as his skillful fingers glided to the back of her neck, massaging, hitting just the right pressure points. His easy charm and champion white-toothed smile smacked her hard in the chest.

With his gaze on hers, he went on. "Hey, I'm not mad at you, bro." He bent and took her mouth again, holding her at the nape, steady as his tongue leisurely toyed with hers, then pulled away and faced Jeff with a grin. "I just want to say thanks for the lapse in judgment."

And there it is. He was goading Jeffrey and Tabitha loved every minute of it. Her ex stood there with that lost-dog expression. From here on, whenever she thought of her ex-fiancé, she'd remember this look.

"Well," Jeff muttered and glanced at Sharon, "yeah, we should get going."

"Okay," Tabitha replied with a bright smile. "It was nice meeting you, Sharon."

"You too, Tabitha. Dominic, uh, Dom."

Dominic waved a hand. "You all enjoy this lovely day." He laughed low and sat down across from her.

As the couple headed off, Tabitha heard Jeffrey grumble to Sharon for salivating over Dominic. In response, Sharon shoved and questioned him about being previously engaged.

"Thanks," she said to Dominic.

He took a sip of her coffee. "I didn't like the way that bastard was taunting you. I caught some of the conversation before I walked up." He leaned forward—smooth-shaven and smelling of a really nice soap—and crossed his forearms on the edge of the table.

"How did you know I was here?"

"I've missed you." He took her hand and adjusted the bracelet at her wrist. "Glad to see you're still wearing it."

Her heart flipped and fluttered, yet she shrugged off the sentiment.

He sighed. "I went by the store. Evie said you'd taken the day off. Then I stopped by your place. I needed to fuel up and was across the street when I spotted you. I wanted to let you know I forwarded our marriage certificate to the attorney. I should hear back in about a week or two."

"Okay."

"I also want to apologize again for what happened in Vegas."

She shook her head. "I don't want to talk about that right now. I...I have some things to work out." Her friends' counseling had provoked a heavy dose of anxiety and also a level of clarity she was still struggling to face.

"Understood. Now, I have to ask—when were you engaged to that chump, Jeffrey? He doesn't strike me as your type."

"So you think you know my type now?"

He sat up, stretched his arms out wide, and smiled just as wide. "Yes, I believe I do." Sobering, he leaned forward again. "But seriously, when?"

"About a year and a half ago."

"Why didn't you go through with it?"

"We argued…" Tabitha cleared her throat. She decided to skip the sordid details and jumped to the end. "He cheated three days before the wedding."

He pushed back against the chair. "Damn. What an asshole. I meant what I said. It's his loss. He didn't deserve you."

She dropped her gaze to her coffee cup. The warmth seen in his eyes mixed with the sincerity in his voice struck the tumultuous cord of her emotions.

He took her hand that rested on the table and pressed a kiss across her knuckles. "The trust matter, I can't thank you enough for what you've done for me."

The tenderness in his touch, the sweetness in his tone, the scent of his skin, it all pitched her back to the drugging pleasures of their time spent in Vegas. She'd missed him too.

Tabitha withdrew her hand, yet her skin still tingled where his soft lips had been. She came to her feet, and he followed suit. "I should get home to shower and change. My brother, Troy, is having a party this afternoon."

"Maybe I could join you. Meet the fam." They walked

the short distance to their cars parked side by side. "For all intents and purposes, we're married." He grinned. "You're Mrs. Balaska."

She drew back. "You do realize we'll be getting a divorce the second the ink dries on your trust fund distribution." A soft frown creased his brow. They were married, yes, but she wasn't about to make it that easy.

"I'm aware. But until then…" He looked down at himself. "Will this do?"

She regarded his clothes. At the very least, having him at the party would keep whichever guy Troy had lined up off her back. "It's a T-shirt and shorts kind of shindig. And there will be plenty of food. Even enough to conquer your elephant-size appetite." That grin of his went wide. The man was incorrigible. And wickedly gorgeous. And able to send her heart into a strange pitter-patter. "The party is supposed to start in the late afternoon. Troy's coming off a night rotation at the firehouse. He'll likely sleep until noon. Change and meet at my house around four."

"I'll be there."

Chapter Seventeen

T HE DOORBELL RANG. *Right on time.* Tabitha jogged downstairs and pulled open the door. Dominic cradled a brown paper bag. "What's that?" She stepped aside, and he sauntered across the threshold but stopped short when Dixie hopped in his path. Percy was right on her tail.

Tabitha scooped them up. "Meet my babies. This is Dixie. And this one's Percy."

"Not into dogs or cats?"

She almost took offense, but he reached out and tenderly stroked their heads. "They were a gift from Jeff…about the only positive that came out of that wasted three years of my life." She placed the pair into their cage tucked on the side of the couch.

"Having met the man, I'll save the *why him* for another day. I bought beer." He set the bag on the table.

She was definitely happy to shove Jeff in her rearview mirror. "That wasn't necessary."

"I'm Greek. It's almost a sin to show up empty-handed to a party."

"I'm sure it'll get swallowed up." She crossed to the kitchen to get the pesto pasta salad she'd whipped up to take with them.

"These, however, are for you. Thought we could christen our arrangement, not that we didn't do a thorough job the night following our nuptials."

Tabitha turned around from the fridge and made a slight hitch in surprise. He held in one hand a bottle of Cristal and in the other, multicolored flowers wrapped in protective pink tissue paper. Her silence must have gone on too long because he circled the center island and came up to her. The hard somersault her stomach took brought about momentary nausea as she stared at his outstretched hands. "We don't have to do that."

"No, we don't. However, I'd like us to."

She set the bowl on the counter and took the flowers before retrieving two wineglasses. As he poured, she filled a vase with water, trimmed the ends off the stems, and put the beautiful arrangement in it while using the small reprieve to calm her jitters. Then she accepted the glass he patiently held out to her.

"Thank you for being my temporary wife." He took large swallows, quickly emptying the glass.

She tasted a small sip. Then he took her glass and placed it with his on the counter. Before she could react, his hands caught her waist and drew her in, her breasts to the hard plane of his chest.

"Dominic, what are you doing?"

"We could finish it off with a kiss." His voice was low, husky. A hand skimmed across her ass. The heat of his palm scorched through her shorts.

She moistened her lips, recalling how soft and warm his felt pressed against hers. "Look, this married thing is on paper only." She stepped out of his embrace, and an immediate coolness licked her exposed limbs. "Sex isn't part of the deal."

His brow rose. "Why not? Did you forget Vegas? We've already had sex, so what's the issue?"

"What happened in Vegas, stays in Vegas." As she placed the champagne in the fridge and grabbed the salad, those words needed to run on a reel to not forget. He was charming. And hot. And sexy. And amazing in bed. She could lose herself in him if she wasn't careful. She headed for the door but glanced back when he didn't follow. "You coming with me or what?"

"We tend to do that pretty on point together." He grinned as his gaze swept unapologetically up and down her body. "Wouldn't you agree?"

Tabitha swallowed a small pant. "Let's go. And you're driving."

TROY'S HOME HAD been a flip. He'd purchased it at an auction and did most of the restoration himself. The small split level sat off the main two-lane stretch of private road within a nestle of tall, aged trees. Behind a meticulously landscaped front yard, the whitewashed brick structure backed up to an open field where electrical towers stood. County ordinance prevented any construction beyond the wide field of property.

Vehicles butted front to back along the spacious cemented side yard. Tabitha had Dominic park behind the minivan of Troy's wife, Rena, in the long, narrow driveway.

She checked her appearance in the car's sun visor. With the early evening temperature hovering around a comfortable seventy-six degrees, she'd insisted they ride with the top down.

"Here." Dominic tucked loose strands that had escaped her braid back behind her ears, the tips of his fingers taking liberty on down her neck. "Oh, and I still want that kiss."

Tabitha ignored him as she gathered up the pasta bowl on her lap and pushed open the car door. He jogged around the front of the sleek black sports car and took her hand to help her out of the low-profile seat, then grabbed the bag of beer she'd stationed on the floor between her legs.

Music and the smell of seasoned grilled meat guided them into the house and down the stairs to the kitchen. Rena looked up from her bent position by the door. A kind smile lit her attractive African-Cuban features as she hurried forward to greet them. Tabitha wasn't as much of a hugger as her sister in-law tended to be. Aware, Rena made it quick.

"Tab! So glad you made it." Her attention shifted to Dominic, and that smile stretched practically from ear to ear. "And who might you be?"

"This is Dominic Balaska, a, uh, colleague of mine." His head rotated to her. She ignored his questioning look as he shook Rena's hand.

"Hope you don't mind me tagging along."

"No! My goodness, not at all! I'm glad to have you." She gave a nod at the bag. "You didn't have to bring anything."

"It's just beer. Where should I put it?"

"That ice chest there by the door. I was about to wheel it

outside. John and Craig should be back with more ice any minute."

When he turned away, Rena smiled and silently mouthed *he's hot* with two thumbs up.

Tabitha rolled her eyes. "As requested, I made my pasta salad." She set the bowl among the horde of other eats on the table.

"Ooh, thank you so much. Dominic, have you had Tab's pasta salad? It's to die for. I've tried to make it and have yet to get it right. Troy does the cooking in this house."

"No. I'll have to try it."

"You'll need to get in line. All of us here love her salad, practically anything she makes. Tab, bring it out back." Rena gestured at the overpacked kitchen table. "This spread is the overflow from the stash outside. Dominic, I'll introduce you to the gang."

Rena led the way beyond the opened French doors to the patio. Conversations were noticeably muted among the thirty or so people laughing and lounging about on sunny orange, deep-cushioned lawn furniture.

"That's my brother, Benito, and his girlfriend, Maggie." Rena pointed to the couple seated together on one of the chaises.

"The two there at the table, Max and Brady with Mark and Jim playing spades and those two over there, Derrick and Tom, are Troy's firefighter buddies."

Tabitha observed the many scrutinizing looks as a general *hello* came from everyone. Aside from firefighters Max, Brady, Derrick, and Tom, the rest were a sea of black and brown familiar faces. She said quick hellos to several people she knew as they made their way over to Troy at the grill.

"Troy, this is Tabitha's colleague, Dominic."

Troy stepped away from the sizzling meat and shook his hand. "Hope you're hungry."

"Troy and I are twins—fraternal, of course," Tabitha said, noticing Dominic's study of them.

"Who brought the imported stuff?"

Their heads turned in the direction of a deep baritone voice. Hair neatly trimmed high and tight, deep chocolate eyes, and angled features—the ebony hottie who stepped out of the house carrying the ice chest instead of rolling it gave Tabitha momentary pause before she recognized him. Craig Morrison. She glanced at Dominic and saw him staring at her dead-on, a slight furrow marring an otherwise smooth brow.

"I'm more interested in who owns that sick-ass drop-top parked in the driveway."

Tabitha's head turned again, and she caught sight of her brother, John, striding a few paces behind Craig. She hadn't seen John in nearly two months. Landscaper entrepreneur, he'd been working on a multimillion-dollar, ten-acre spread down in Atlanta.

Her brothers looked out for her. Where Troy would be considered the easygoing one, John had always been her protector. After her ordeal with Jeff, her eldest brother became even more wary of any man she met…that he hadn't vetted first.

She planted her sneakered feet solidly on the gray flag-stone as he strutted forward and wrapped her into a tight, warm hug.

"Hey, lady. Troy didn't think you were coming. You have to get out of that store more often during the day to get some sun. We're starting to not look like we share the same DNA."

Unlike her and Troy's warm tan skin tone, John was more medium brown. But it was his rich whiskey-brown eyes that held women transfixed. That and his boisterous charisma.

"This is Dominic. He's a colleague of Tab's," Rena said before Tabitha had a second to do the honors. "The car out front is his."

The men shook hands.

"You're riding around like Tony Stark up in here." John laughed.

Dominic chuckled, apparently catching the *Iron Man* reference. "I also brought the imported," he said to Craig before gripping palms with him, too.

"Good choice on the beer." Craig turned to Tabitha and gave her a lingering hug. "Hey, lady, it's been a while. How have you been?"

"I'm good. I thought you were working in New England."

"Craig recently transferred to the firehouse," Troy remarked over his shoulder as he tended to the meat.

"What he said." Craig grinned. "I mentioned I wanted to come back to the area. There was an opening at his station." He took her hand. "Do you still hit the trails? I actually had a good time when you dragged me out there."

"And you complained the entire time." Both laughed lightly. "I've been busy at the bakery."

"Yeah, I hear things are good. Troy was telling me about all that you have going. If anyone can hold it down, you can. We'll have to catch up."

Tabitha turned her head toward Dominic. His steady stare spoke louder than any words would. She detached her hand from Craig's and slipped her fingers between Dominic's, hoping to solidify their understanding. "I'm hungry. Let's get something to eat."

"I have your steaks right here." Troy grabbed sturdy paper plates from a stack and delivered up two juicy sirloins for her and Dominic. "Enjoy."

Tabitha eyed the hefty portion on their way to the smorgasbord of covered Tupperware. "This is far too much meat for me. I'll finish maybe a corner."

"Here." Dominic grabbed a knife from a canister of utensils, sliced off about three-quarters of her steak, and forked it onto his plate. "How's that?"

"Good. Thanks."

They each went for the crisp mixed greens, cucumber and tomato slices, and sweet corn salad. He lifted the lid to the pasta dish she'd brought and faced an empty bowl. "Seriously?! Your sister in-law wasn't kidding."

"Nope. I'll have to make a batch just for you." She regarded him. His expression was severely neutral. "Try this. It's bacon beer mac-and-cheese. Troy does this right." She spooned a heaping amount onto his plate, then asked, "What do you want to drink?"

"Some of the imported stuff?" A faint smile.

She grabbed the beer and got a carbonated water for herself. They sat at a table and ate in comfortable silence for a good stretch of time. Benito's mixed beats made their heads bob. Some responded to the rhythmic tempo with bodies swaying, others continued to chatter.

Tabitha observed that Dominic's plate was practically empty. "If I ate as much as you, I wouldn't be able to fit through the door," she joked and received a hint of a shrug.

"Fast metabolism. I trust we still have an agreement. I'm a man of my word. Can I count on you to do the same? Or do I need to put a ring on it?"

The comment came out of left field. "What is that supposed to mean? Nothing has changed between this morning and now."

"You're sure about that? Since apparently you don't intend to tell your family about our arrangement, a courtesy heads-up would be nice before you go out on dates."

Tabitha read the bristling undercurrent in his tone and followed his stare over to where Craig stood with her brothers. The three, along with a group of others, were in a pack-like huddle, laughing it up. The trio's heads seemed to turn as one toward them. Troy jogged over. "John and I are picking teams for flag football. Tab, you're on my team."

"I don't get a say?"

"Nope. You have to block Rena on John's team. Dominic, you in?"

Tabitha looked at him in his Nats T-shirt, cargo shorts, and sockless feet within tan boat shoes. "You don't have to play. Besides, you're not dressed for it."

Dominic came to his feet. "My gym bag is in the car. Give me five to change."

OUT IN THE open field, Dominic rolled, flexed, and stretched his muscles. A short distance away, Tabitha stood among her brothers and the others on her team. His gaze swept over long, toned arms and legs. She looked his way and sent a small smile. The sight of it made his heart do its familiar flutter.

He was aware she'd been quizzically watching him with side glances. He also caught her doing the same to Craig when she didn't think Dominic was paying attention. To say it didn't bother him would be a bald-faced lie. He couldn't make sense of the sudden rise of possessiveness he felt. Nor could he explain it to her. Both understood their involvement had an end date.

Dominic looked on as Tabitha and Craig chatted. He held on to his restraint as he witnessed the man slip the corner of a yellow bandanna handkerchief inside the back pocket of her ass-hugging short shorts.

"Let's do this! You're going down, my brother," Troy called with an arrow-straight finger pointed at John, who returned the gesture. Obvious competitors, the two took the roles of quarterback. Everyone got into position.

With the corner of his flag tucked securely in the waistband of his jersey knit shorts, he got low, planting his back foot firmly. John hiked the ball to the guy hunched behind him. As the receiver jogged backward and released the ball like a rocket, Dominic took off and made a quick cross in front of Craig, leaped, and caught the ball on a fast twist, then hauled ass past the cones. Flag untouched.

"Touchdown!" several pseudo refs called out from among those seated beneath the shaded patio. Across the field, his team roared his name and rallied, giving each other high fives.

He inhaled deep and released just as deep to level his breathing. Tabitha walked alongside him. "Somebody's got skills. Didn't know you had it in you, Balaska. You'll have to join me sometime when I run the ten."

He returned her grin. "I'm up for that."

She jogged backward. "That's one way…just so you know." She winked. Craig called her name, momentarily drawing her attention with a look over her shoulder. "Dom, your sneaker's untied."

It was the first time he ever recalled hearing her using his nickname. Well, she had at Dabney's during her little performance. She whirled and caught up with the other man. On her approach, Craig threw his head back in deep laughter at something she said and gave her a light shoulder shove. The man seemed to easily find her comfort zone. Having an in with her brothers surely gave him an advantage.

She'd re-erected that solid wall between them, one that had been damn near impossible to break down the first time, and he anticipated another round of him going all uphill.

They got into formation again. John took several broad backward hops to avoid Troy charging at him. He released the ball. Tabitha banked right and caught it. Dominic took pleasure in watching her athleticism, moving about with confident agility.

He got his head back into the game and moved in, but Craig came at her from the left. She cradled the ball close to her chest with a quick duck and dodge. Craig captured her hips, his body melded against hers. She laughingly squirmed as he reached around and snagged her flag. They lost their footing with her landing ass-flat, the two in a tangled sprawl upon the freshly cut grass.

"Penalty on the play," Troy laughingly shouted before Dominic could grit the words out. "This isn't a contact sport."

Nor was the game called Feel Her Up, but the dude had managed to do that quite thoroughly.

As they sorted into position once more, Dominic crossed to Tabitha. She was hardly out of breath. "You okay?" He pulled a fleck of green earth from her mussed hair. He wanted to tell her to sit this one out, but that would be pointless.

"I'm fine." She squinted and blocked the sun from her eyes with the edge of her hand. "But my ass will be sore tomorrow." She laughed. "That fluffy grass is deceiving."

He retrieved his Ray-Bans from his pocket and slipped them on her while leaning in near her ear. "If you recall, I have a remedy for that."

One eyebrow merely lifted, her expression hidden behind the smoke-colored lenses.

Craig smacked his hands together. "Are we going to play or what?"

Definitely a tactic to separate them.

In position, Troy released the ball. His teammate made the catch, ran the yards, and scored. Rena intercepted the next play. She took off a good distance before Troy caught her but graciously didn't remove her flag, settling for a kiss instead. Everyone laughingly shouted *penalty on the play*, but they dismissed the call and waited for them to break the lip-lock that held for long seconds. The last two plays tied the game with John in possession of the ball.

Dominic caught up with Tabitha. "When I break the tie here in a minute, how about that kiss I asked for earlier?"

"*When* you break it? Pretty sure of yourself." She laughed. "*If* that happens, your team wins. Why would I want to reward you?"

He shrugged a shoulder. "Call it a way of reinforcing our arrangement."

Her brow furrowed. "I'm a woman of my word. I said I'd help you get your trust. You don't have to be concerned." She jogged on.

It wasn't about the damn trust. It was about the suddenly barbaric possessiveness he felt. Seeing her rubbing up with Craig had tossed his feelings about her into an unfamiliar place.

He dragged his gaze away from her to try to focus on the game in play. The ball came at him like a bullet. He wasn't quite in position. Craig leaped in front of him, clipping Dominic's shin. The collision sent them both to the ground like heavy stones. The throbbing in his ankle started almost instantly. An interception made for an easy score. Shouts, laughter, high fives, and cheers mingled.

Dominic stared up for a moment at a spinning, waning prism of dusky sky and low clouds as he worked to catch his breath, then slowly came to his feet.

Teammates on both sides surrounded them and offered pats on the back, then made a beeline for the patio. Beer, water, and soda became their narrow focus.

Lights flickered on, illuminating the plush green land-scape and well-placed flagstone. The music turned up, courtesy of Benito's DJ skills. Heads bobbed. Some snagged partners and rocked out on beat.

The barest pressure on his right leg provoked a sharp twinge at his ankle. Dominic worked to put as little weight on the limb as possible.

"Sorry about that, my man," Craig said, keeping a slow pace beside him. "All in the name of fun, right?"

The guy had clipped him but good. Whether accidental or on purpose, he couldn't quite determine, but Craig was mocking. As Tabitha approached, Dominic slowed his already sluggard stride.

"You boys okay?" She took off his sunglasses and hung them in the V of her T-shirt, between her breasts. "I can attest that ground is rock solid. I think we'll all have nice bruises tomorrow."

"All good on this end," Craig assured, chest puffed pea-cock wide.

"And you?" She eyed Dominic closely.

"Same." He continued forward, but she stopped him with a light touch on his arm. "I saw that. You're limping. Where does it hurt?"

Around the curve of my pride right about now. He glanced at Craig over by the ice chest of imported beers. A soft grin played across the man's mouth. The dirty field move had been done on purpose, and it spoke volumes. Craig saw him as competition. An inward satisfaction sizzled like revitalizing fuel.

"We're leaving." Anxious concern colored the rosy glow of Tabitha's sun-drenched face. "Give me a minute. I'll let my family know." She pivoted.

"No." Dominic caught her arm, and she turned back. "I'm good." *Your brothers aren't about to call me a pussy. Fuck that.* She continued to look him over with a scrutinizing eye. "Will you kiss it and make it better?" he said with a wolfish smile.

The worried expression left her face. She delivered that slow roll of her eyes that always managed to provoke a snugness within his boxer briefs.

"Sit your butt down somewhere while I get you some ice for your leg."

"Tabitha, I'm fine." He caught her wrist again, stalling her determined stride. "Really, I'm good. I'll soak in the tub later."

"You're sure?"

Drawing her braid over her shoulder, he said softly, "If I didn't know better, I'd think you care about me."

"I do care about you." Long, dark lashes fluttered. "I-I mean I don't like seeing anyone in discomfort."

"Of course."

She started forward again but stopped and turned sharply. "What are you doing later?"

He shrugged. "Like I said, sitting in the tub."

"How about we do that together at my place?"

Mixed signals, though he wasn't about to split hairs. "I can do that."

She took her phone from her back pocket and gave him a sly side look, lips curving upward. "I'll text Carlos to have him open the store in the morning, since I anticipate being in later than usual."

Dominic's grin stretched even farther. "Most definitely. You do that."

They strode to the patio. Both cleaned their hands with a couple of wet wipes stationed on the table, then went to where Rena stood setting out desserts. Her warm smile greeted them.

Dominic surveyed the assortment of cakes, brownies, pie slices, and a host of just about every cookie choice imaginable. "I don't know where to start. Everything looks delicious."

"I'm lucky to have a sister in-law who co-owns a bakery. It's some of Chase Confections's finest," Rena said.

He snagged a chocolate fudge cookie from the tray, prepared to devour it whole, but it was snatched from his hand.

"You can't eat that." Tabitha took a bite. "It has peanut butter slivers in it. He's allergic," she told Rena. "Everything else should be okay. Try these. It's one of our newest. I know how much you like blueberries."

Dominic leaned in and took a bite of the cake square she fed him. He moaned in delight.

"Good, right?" She popped the rest into her mouth. "I've been playing around with new recipes. Here, you have…" She brushed away the crumbs at the corner of his lip with her thumb, handed him a beer, and then finished off the peanut butter-infused cookie.

He ate another cake square. "This is really good. You should add it to Pearl's menu."

"What is it with you and blueberries?" Tabitha laughed

lightly and shook her head. Rena stood staring at them, smiling.

The music's upbeat tempo was replaced by a more crooning harmony, bringing couples hip to hip.

"There's my lovely wife." Troy took Rena in his arms, and the two blended in among the throng.

Dominic caught sight of Craig making his way toward Tabitha. He quickly grabbed her hand and was pleased when she didn't object. Instead, her fingers easily closed around his. "Dance with me, beautiful."

She smiled. "What about your leg?"

"All good." He lightly tugged her in front of him. With his hands fitted to the soft curves of her hips, he guided her toward those gyrating and swaying. She turned and circled her arms around his neck. His eyes on hers, he brought her in close, their bodies nearly touching, and let the cadence of the seductive sound guide their rhythm. Their gazes held; no words were spoken as they studied each other.

"Dom, I see you're full of surprises this evening. You can handle a football. And I see you know how to groove. I'm impressed."

"There's a lot about me you don't know. And I like it when you call me that." He was enjoying her delicate fingers playing in the hairs at the nape of his neck.

"Maybe I'll use it more often," she said softly, displaying that heart-stopping smile.

He took note of John's keen eyes tracking them while pretending to nurse a beer. A few steps away, dancing with her husband, Rena watched them as well. He reciprocated her smile, then brought his gaze back to Tabitha. *What would her family do if I kissed her right here?* He longed for a taste of her. "I'll be heading back to Vegas on Monday to finish up some work and for several meetings I rescheduled when I left prematurely."

She nodded. "Have you told Trenton about our arrangement?"

"Yes, and to say he wanted to kick my ass would be putting it mildly. I was lectured on the many reasons why it wasn't a smart move." Her brow creased slightly "My brother doesn't want to see you get hurt." She went still, even seemed to be holding her breath. A few light strokes at her back got their sway back on beat. "Trent also fears that it could, in essence, jeopardize his relationship with Kennedi." He coaxed her in a bit closer. "I would never hurt you, Tabitha. Know that." He purposely spoke with firm certainty.

There was no shift in her expression, not even the slightest twitch. "You've apparently told Kennedi, and I would assume Evie also."

"Yes. Since Evie's separation from her husband, her creed has been 'live and let live.' Kennedi, she's more the 'reserve judgment' sort. Overall, both are supportive in their own way."

"You'll tell your business partners about our arrangement but not your family?" Her fingers left his hair, making him regret the argument.

"I'd rather not, that's all. It's not like we'll be married for long, so what would be the point?"

The music faded, leaving dead air. She hadn't stepped out of his arms for more than mere seconds before John called out to her. Their heads turned to Craig and him standing among a small circle of people. Her brother beckoned with a stiff bend of fingers. Dominic read Tabitha's slight hesitation. "Go. I should get off this ankle for a bit."

"I'll be right back." She trotted off.

"Benito, what happened to the music?" Rena asked. Her brother jumped to attention, jetting into the house. Within minutes, the backyard party vibe picked up a second wind, sweeping on a warm current of soft melody.

Dominic took note of John's overt intent to pin his sister to Craig, despite the fact that Tabitha hadn't arrived at the party alone. Their marriage license notwithstanding, aside from their arrangement, he and she had no real tie to one another. That fact didn't wash away the offense.

He got himself a couple of cinnamon cookies and took a seat at the foot of a lounger. Elbows on his knees, he munched and enjoyed observing Tabitha with her family and friends, how relaxed and content she seemed, enough to even have invited him over later to share a bathtub with her. Her easy laughter reverberated through him like warm waves. He loved seeing this side of her, free of all barriers.

I love her.

His heart did a strange flip. The last thing he wanted to do was take that joy away from her, and he couldn't condemn her for relishing Craig's familiar company. Trenton was right—he should never have involved her in the trust matter. He should have found another way or nothing at all. How would he let go when his heart was now dug in so deep?

Rena stepped into his narrow line of view and took a seat

beside him.

"How long have you two been dating?"

He turned his head and met kind, doe-brown eyes. Though straight to the point, she'd whispered the words with a glance across the patio at her husband and brother in-law. The two hovered over their sister like protective hawks as Tabitha chatted with Craig and a few others. "We're not dating." They were legally married, but that wasn't something he could share.

"Right. You're *colleagues*." Hard air quotes. Rena sucked her teeth. "Even though you're the first man in a long time she's brought within a hundred feet of her brothers. The way she looks at you… Hell, the way you look at each other…"

Dominic's stomach tightened unexpectedly. Tabitha wanted to keep what little connection they shared private. "You're misreading it."

"If you say so." Her expression grew somber. "After what that asshole ex of hers—" She paused on a sigh. "Just know I'm glad you're here. It's a good sign."

"I presume you're referring to that chump, Jeff."

Her eyes widened a touch. "She told you about him? Wow, she must really like you. We're not allowed to even speak his name in her presence."

Dominic flinched a little. According to Kennedi, Tabitha had once given him that treatment, too. "I met him. Sort of came upon him."

"Then you know he's a piece of garbage." A scowl hardened her delicate features. "The fact that he would cheat on her after everything she went through. He knew her health was fragile during that time."

"No joke."

"But she got through it. Then to lose the baby so soon after beating ovarian cancer. She was devastated. When I saw her in that hospital bed…" She shook her head with a look over at Tabitha, affection surfacing in her warm eyes.

He was aware Tabitha had suffered from ovarian cancer and was once engaged. But now learning the child she'd miscarried was for that piece of shit, Jeff, fuck, she'd been through hell for sure. It explained why she guarded her trust with an iron shield.

"I understand why she'd want to keep your relationship from those two. Mainly John." Rena tipped her head in the direction of the Seils brothers. "That said, it appears Craig's their pick for her this round. They know him; there's history there. And they see him as the complete opposite end of the spectrum from Jeff."

"Because he's African-American?" *Can't compete with that. Not that I am. Am I?* Dominic held her stare.

"Craig's race might play a small part, but mainly it's because he's not an ego-headed, money-grabbing prick."

Dominic winced. According to Trent, Tabitha had once said similar things about him. The arrangement he'd made with her regarding the trust pretty much locked him into that last attribute.

"Craig's an army reservist slash firefighter, and from the little I know, he does fine financially. That's not to say you… Obviously, you're… What I mean is, he's someone John feels he can trust."

"From where I sit, Tabitha seems to be able to hold her own."

"Yes, I agree. She takes care of herself just fine. That said, her brothers believe if they choose a guy for her, she won't get hurt again. I've told them that's not how it works, but the mere notion gives them peace of mind."

Dominic watched as Tabitha took her phone from her back pocket and Craig tapped away on his. Clearly, they were exchanging information. The man was friends with her brothers. And from the looks of it, she and Craig had easily reacquainted as well.

Rena touched his arm. He met her soft gaze and warm countenance. Both looked across the patio. "Know that they mean well. Their baby sister is the sun, moon, and stars in their eyes."

The siblings teased one another with boisterous bouts of laughter. He actually respected John and Troy for the amount of love they had for their sister.

He came to his feet. The sting in his ankle took him slightly off-balance. Dancing probably hadn't been a good idea.

Rena angled her head, studying his rapidly swelling and reddening bruise. "You really should put some ice on that. I'll get it for you." She snapped to her feet.

"Nah, I'm good." He rotated his foot. Stiffness had already started to set in. "Mind if I use the facility?"

"Up the stairs on your right."

After a quick trip to the bathroom, he reversed his steps back to the kitchen.

A young woman was there tidying up. She tried to balance a stack of containers cradled in her arms on her way to the fridge. One of her cargo started to slip free. "Whoa."

Dominic caught it. "Here you go."

"Great reflexes. Thanks. That coleslaw would've been a mess to clean up." They stacked the food in the fridge. "By the way, I'm Gayle, Rena's cousin."

"Dominic."

"You're pretty quick with a football too. I watched you play."

"Then you watched me land flat on my ass."

"Ouch." She laughed. "That I did. But you even made that look good." Her eyes dipped slowly downward and she gave him an overt once-over while wearing an appreciative smile. "Dominic, is there anything I can get you?"

Okay. At another time in his life, not so long ago, getting hit on by a beautiful woman at a party would've resulted in the two of them finding a hideaway and fucking their brains out. Now, his bogus marriage to Tabitha weighed as heavily as any legit bond real couples shared. It was ridiculous to think or even expect Tabitha would treat their arrangement the same. Still...

"No, but thank you."

"I thought you left."

Dominic whirled around to find John standing at the threshold, assessing him and Gayle with a dissecting thoroughness. "Nah, still here. Just a trip to the bathroom."

John moved to the deep freezer in the corner and took from it a bag of ice. "You don't have to stick around. I'll take Tab home. When the three of us get together, no telling how late it'll be."

"Don't you mean the four of you?" Dominic smiled mildly, meeting him eye to eye. "We arrived together. It's fitting that I see her home."

"Look, my man, she's enjoying herself. No sense in you hanging around. I don't get to see my sister that often. We each have busy schedules, businesses to run. You understand. Like I said, I'll take her home when she's ready."

The edge in his tone suggested it wasn't up for debate. Dominic more than understood the dynamics playing out. The last thing he wanted was to make himself an enemy of this guy. Yet... He turned to Gayle. "It was nice meeting you."

"You too."

He left the kitchen. Short steps away, he found Tabitha with Craig. The pair stood intimately close. Craig's hand rested on the small curve of her spine.

Dominic shouldn't have asked to join her here. What was the point? They weren't a real couple. But he wanted to know more about her, had been desperate to catch another glimpse of the compassionate, passionate woman she'd allowed him to see back in Vegas. "Tabitha?" Both turned almost as one. He realized they'd been looking at something on Craig's phone.

"Dominic." A smile brightened her already lovely features. "Craig was showing—"

"I'm going to head out," he cut in, not interested in anything related to Craig.

"Oh. Okay. I'll grab my purse."

"No, you stay. Hang out with your family. Thanks for the invite." He looked at Craig and the two gave a nod. No sense in pretending. Then he pivoted and started toward the brightly lit flagstone path on the side of the house that led to the front driveway.

"Dominic?" Quick footsteps followed. "Dom?"

He turned, and Tabitha damn near ran into him.

"I said give me a minute to let everyone know I'm leaving. I'll meet you at the car."

"Tabitha, stay and enjoy your family. It's all good." He continued on.

"Well, you can't go anywhere without your car key," she called.

Right. He'd asked her to put his fob in her purse before they played football. Turning again, he followed her back into the kitchen. Gayle and John were still there. Both seemed to be heavily involved in a deep discussion; John's disappointment at seeing him didn't go unnoticed.

Tabitha grabbed her purse off the top of the fridge and handed him his fob. Soft fingers slipped into his palm and entwined with his. "I thought you and I...we had plans later," she said quietly with a subtle glance over her shoulder at her brother.

Her affectionate behavior took him a bit by surprise, a side of her he seldom witnessed. But with reluctance, he released her hand. "Enjoy your family." He cast a glance at John behind her. "I'll call you, Tabitha." The sour look her brother delivered him was one for the record book.

She reared back, her features pinched. "You'll call me... Uh, okay."

"Have a good evening, all."

"Don't forget your sunglasses."

Dominic paused on his stride to the stairs and gave a look over his shoulders.

She snatched them from the perfect V of her shirt and shoved them out to him.

"Keep them. They look good on you."

Chapter Eighteen

"WHAT IN THE hell just happened?" Tabitha felt the door slam shut on any involvement with Dominic beyond their arrangement as sure as the entry door had on his way out. She swung her head from Gayle to John, back and forth. "Somebody had better start talking."

"All I said was I'd take you home. You're so busy at the bakery, I never see you. Is it wrong of me to want to spend a little time with my baby sister?"

"No, but you and I both know that's not why you want me here and wanted Dominic gone. You and Troy need to cool it with these setups. I'm doing fine on my own."

"If you mean Dominic, he was in here playing get-to-know-you with Gayle."

Tabitha pivoted her head back to the woman hemmed against the fridge as a swift wave of possessiveness clouded rational reasoning. "Gayle, what is he talking about? Were you trying to get with my guy?"

"I thought *your guy* was outside."

Just then, Troy strode into the kitchen. Rena and Craig trailed behind him. "Dude, where's the ice?" Reading the tense faces, Troy recoiled. "What's going on?"

John scowled at Tabitha. "What do you mean, your

guy?"

"You heard me. Dominic and I are lovers. There, I said it." They were also husband and wife, but why give her brothers a heart attack? *Tackle one battle at a time.*

"I knew it!"

Tabitha ignored Rena. "You and Troy can stop interfering in my love life. I've got it covered. Thanks." She stared back at their opened mouths while waiting for her heart rate to adjust. The thought that Dominic Balaska had just walked out of her life right when she'd realized how much he meant to her threw her into a paralyzing state of panic. She yanked her phone from her back pocket and sent off a text:

Sorry about my brothers. They can be overbearing pains in the ass.

As she waited and waited and waited, she paced in a tight circle through several rapid heartbeats.

No reply.

THE UBER DRIVER dropped Tabitha off at the curb of her driveway. She marched straight inside, upstairs, stripped, and got into the shower, hoping it would help tame her distressed mood. She'd left Troy's house so damn angry with John, she had to get out of there.

As she stood before the bathroom mirror and combed out the knotted tangles, then braided and tied her damp hair beneath a satin scarf, she couldn't help wondering who took precedence, who did Dominic consider more important than spending the night with her. Was he seeing someone else?

He did have options. She'd witnessed them firsthand.

She grabbed her phone from the nightstand on her climb into bed. Dominic had yet to reply to her text message. Even when they weren't on good terms, he'd always responded. She whipped off another text:

Hey, I'm home. Can't sleep. That invite is still open.

Dominic: I'm in for the night.

There were very few reasons a man would refuse an invitation to spend the night with a woman: either he simply wasn't interested in her, or the bed space beside him was already occupied.

How about breakfast tomorrow morning?

His reply came almost simultaneously as she hit send.

Preparing for my trip. But thanks.

Stunned, she still asked: *What did my brother say to you? Come over so we can talk.*

Tabitha, it's all good. I'm headed to bed. Take care of yourself. Good night.

What in all the hell…?

She stared at her phone, completely flummoxed. What exactly might John have said to flip Dominic's switch?

COME OVER SO we can talk.

Stretched out between cool sheets, Dominic tossed his phone on the other side of the bed and grabbed the TV remote from the nightstand, followed by his half-finished glass of Maker's Mark. It took all he had not to go to her. The ache in his chest, the sensation was so profound, he could barely draw a full breath.

He'd had a taste of her in Vegas, unguarded, and wanted more of that. The heart-churning, raw emotional upset he now felt was his own doing. He should never have involved her in helping to solve his trust issue in the first place.

Now, knowing all Tabitha had gone through with her ex, he understood why she wanted to keep their arrangement from her family. It also explained why her brothers kept a protective pack-like huddle around her. To shield her from people like him. He couldn't fault them for that. To selfishly try to push his way beyond those gates would cause a fracture within her family and frustrate him.

He knew what he needed to do, but he wasn't ready to face the heart-crushing conclusion.

Chapter Nineteen

T HE CLOCK CRAWLED toward one a.m. by the time exhaustion conquered Tabitha's racing thoughts. A mere five hours later, she headed to work. Carlos greeted her in the kitchen.

"Thanks for opening up." She grabbed an apron from the wall hook on her way to the back office to deposit her purse and keys in the drawer. She caught her reflection in the small mirror hanging by the door. Puffy eyes, a telltale sign of having had little to no sleep.

"Anytime. But I thought you weren't coming in until later."

"My plans changed."

Dominic's dismissal continued to plague and gnaw at her. By noon she'd checked her phone at least ten times in hopes of any communication from him, but to no avail. The day wore on, and that evening, lying in bed, unable to wait him out any longer, she broke down and texted.

How's your leg?

She stared at the phone, waiting for a reply. The ring gave her a start. Her stomach lurched and tightened as she opened the line to Dominic. "Hey."

"Evening. The leg's better. Thanks for asking."

"That's good. All set for your trip? You leave tomorrow."

"Yes." He was silent for a moment. "I've decided not to move forward with the trust."

Tabitha tensed. "Why? You'll lose out on getting your money."

"I'm aware. When I return from Vegas, we can get an annulment."

Struggling between what she was sure she heard and what she didn't want to believe, she asked again, "Why?"

"It's what's best," he said in a strange, broken voice.

"For who? Because you said yourself the money will be forfeited back to the trust if you're not married by your birthday. That's been satisfied."

"I still intend to pay you what was agreed upon. I'll settle it when I return."

Puzzled and unbearably wounded by his startlingly abrupt change, she said with a firmness she didn't feel, "Keep it. The money was part of an arrangement we made. If it's no longer in play, you're absolved of any payment owed."

"I'll honor that part of the agreement. You said it'll help with your adoption costs."

"No thanks. Have a safe trip. Good night."

"Tabitha?" He paused. "Good night."

She closed the line then shut her eyes and burrowed into her pillow, bunching and clutching the covers up to her nose as she shook, curled into a tight ball. She tried to stop it but couldn't while willing the tears back. The pain in her heart came in strong waves, only broken by small respites in her recovering breaths. When her back and leg muscles started spasming, she turned over and found it was only two a.m., and she still had a long night in front of her.

The following morning, she awoke with a clearer picture. A breakup—that soul-crushing feeling as though she could no longer breathe easily. She'd been here before.

Heart heavy, she moved about the bakery's kitchen with mechanical efficiency, not really focusing. Throughout the morning she seesawed between sadness that he'd cut things off and anger that she'd allowed her feelings for him to manifest into such precarious, emotional terrain.

The kitchen door swung open, momentarily pulling her out of the dismal tide. Kennedi bustled in with Evie trailing behind by the tug of her hand.

"Tab, glad you're here!" They paused and stared back at her. "What's wrong?"

She worked to erase the anguish from her expression and straightened. "It's Monday. What do you need?"

They came forward. "I need your and Evie's help." Kennedi led them to the office and closed the door. "The engagement dinner Mrs. Shaw is throwing Trenton and me is getting out of control."

"How so?" Tabitha asked.

"Aside from the fact that I didn't want an engagement dinner or party or anything—let me just put that out there—I'd asked her to keep it intimate, small. Just family and maybe close friends. Mrs. Shaw's last text said she has twenty confirmed attendees. Twenty! Apparently, we view small wildly different."

"Kenni, twenty isn't very many people," Evie said.

"I agree," Tabitha told her. "It's actually a comfortable number."

"It should be okay," Evie tried to assure her.

"Fine, I'll let that go, because the major problem is this—Mrs. Shaw knows my mother passed away and wants to also step in to help pick out my wedding dress, assist with planning the wedding, all of it."

"How is that a problem? That's really nice of her," Evie crooned.

"Nice, yes. But again, I'd rather she not." Kennedi pulled her phone from her handbag and held it out for them to view. "This is the dress she wants me to consider."

Tabitha and Evie looked at the picture. "Wow, it's…" Tabitha tried to find delicate words. "It's…"

"Sista girl, that's hideous." Evie didn't bite her tongue. "Not to mention that skirt might require one of those crinolines. How else is it staying in place like that?"

"It's Trenton's grandmother's gown. She'll be at the dinner, by the way. Mrs. Shaw has asked me to come up on Friday for a dress fitting before everyone arrives for dinner on Saturday. It's the first time I'll get to meet her. Well, we've Skyped, but it's the first face-to-face meeting. I don't want to offend her."

"So you want us to offend?" Tabitha asked.

"No, I want you two to offer voices of reason, back me up when I kindly tell her I don't want to wear that dress at my wedding. She's heavily into her family's genealogy and values tradition. Trent said she has traced their family back to the 1700s."

Tabitha recalled that Dominic had shared with her the same about his mother.

Kennedi took hold of their hands, her warm brown eyes

pleading. "Come on. I really need help with this. You both were planning to attend the dinner on Saturday. Mrs. Shaw knows you two are my maids of honor. It won't seem suspect when you arrive on Friday to join me."

"Kenni, we have the store here to run. All of us away at the same time for two days…" Evie tapped her chin in contemplation. "I don't know if that's smart."

"Carlos can handle the kitchen," Kennedi countered. "He's been with us for three years. Tab, he was your apprentice. You trained him well. He graduated culinary school last year with honors. We all know he's been amazing. It's high time we promote him to kitchen manager. And Amy's been holding down the storefront with ease. We can all agree on that, right? They can manage the staff while we're away."

"Carlos has been stellar around here. I don't know what I'd do without him," Tabitha agreed.

"Amy as well," Evie added.

"Then we all agree they should be promoted?" Kennedi looked between them.

"Yes." Both Tabitha and Evie said in concert.

"With that settled, you two can now join me."

"Kenni, I don't know if Tab and me showing up with you would be a good idea. Mrs. Shaw is your future mother in-law. You want to start off on good footing with her," Evie cautioned.

"Wearing that dress at my wedding won't help with that. You said yourself it's hideous. And it's off-white for heaven's sake."

Evie nodded rapidly. "Yes. Okay, I'm in. My aunt has a home in St. Michaels. Maybe I can pay her a visit while I'm there."

They looked at Tabitha.

"I'll be there for the dinner Saturday, but I won't stay. Dominic and I aren't on good terms."

"Maybe this could be an opportunity for you two to work things out. I mean, he did fly all the way here to make amends for his transgressions," Evie said.

"Yes." Kennedi took a seat on the edge of the desk. "I can see he cares about you."

"He wants an annulment…that is, he wants to cancel our arrangement."

"What about his trust? Won't that affect getting his funds?" Evie asked.

"He's aware, but still he wishes to end things between us." The sudden tears that caught in her lashes quickly sent her friends rushing to offer supportive hugs. "We attended Troy's party, and he must have had words with John. I don't know."

She wept against Kennedi's shoulder. Evie quickly snatched tissues from the box on the desk and handed them to her.

As Tabitha dried her eyes, she shared the details of that day, which included her brothers' meddling. Her friends delivered sympathetic looks.

"Dominic called me a short time after and said he wanted an annulment." More tears broke free.

"Tab, I'm sorry." Kennedi wrapped a comforting arm around her shoulders. "I know you agreed to help Dominic with his trust, but I didn't realize your feelings had grown beyond a friendship."

Tabitha wiped her eyes. "I can't even tell you when it happened. I guess it just came on gradually." She looked between her friends. "I love him," she said with heartbreaking humility.

"Men." Evie hugged her once more.

Tabitha cleared her throat and pushed back against more cresting tears. "Maybe it's for the best. Even with or without his trust, he might want kids someday. I wouldn't have been able to give him that. It's likely one of the reasons he ended it." She caught the tears streaming down her cheek with the tissue and took a breath. "I'm fine. Well, I will be," she admitted. "But I'd rather not hang out at his family's home. Besides, I'm meeting with the adoption agency on Friday. The mother has done a preliminary review of the files. I'll know if I made it to the next round, so to speak."

"Of course you did," Kennedi assured her.

"No doubt. She'd be foolish not to pick you," Evie joined in.

Tabitha's chest tightened. She'd needed their comforting, warm support more than she realized. A sense of renewed perseverance bloomed. "I'll come up Friday after my appointment."

"How about I go with you, then we can head to St. Michaels together?" Evie suggested.

"I'd like that."

"We're going to be aunts!" Evie squealed.

Tabitha chuckled past her distressed mood. "Let's hope so."

DOMINIC PICKED UP his desk phone, then hesitated and set the receiver back in place. He wanted to reach out to his brother for advice. Their last conversation nearly a week ago hadn't gone well. As he grabbed the receiver again and dialed, he suspected this one would be no different. A few short rings; the line connected.

"Trent."

"Yeah."

Okay, he'd anticipated the frigidness. "I wanted to let you know I'm getting an annulment…I'm canceling the arrangement with Tabitha."

"Before your trust has been satisfied?"

"Yes." A long pause saturated the line.

"What in the hell is wrong with you? I'm going to assume you've lost your damn common sense!"

His brother's outburst made Dominic jerk the phone away from his ear so as not to lose an eardrum. He placed the desk phone on speaker then came to his feet.

"I knew it was a bad idea for you to drag her into your shit. But your ass did it anyway. Six months until you lose your trust. You wait until close to the last minute to start giving a damn. Then you come up with that ridiculous scheme."

A pained tightness pressed down on Dominic's chest; the pressure forced him to breathe in short pulls. As he listened to his brother's scolding, he shoved his hands into the front pockets of his slacks and looked down upon Vegas's busy city streets from his twenty-second-floor corner office. He'd been fucking miserable from the second he'd ended the last call with Tabitha.

"Then, when shit turns real for her and she starts having feelings for you, you toss her aside," Trent went on. "What, you're going to find someone else you don't have to fully commit to, so you can—?"

"What did you say?" Dominic whirled around and leaned over the phone. "What do you mean, she has feelings for me?"

"Now you want to play dumb. You heard me."

"Trent, what did Kennedi say? Did Tabitha tell her that?"

"What do you think? Well, Kennedi didn't actually tell me. The ladies went bike riding the other day and had returned to my place. I was in my study and overheard them talking in the kitchen. Tabitha touched on her feelings about you."

"You eavesdropped."

"Take the damn information any way you can get it."

Dominic sighed. "You're right. I fucked up." He spilled out all that took place with Tabitha at her brother's home. "Having met her family, the way they look out for her, I can assure you, there's nothing I can say that would convince her brothers that I hadn't been trying to use her by drawing her into my trust issue. There's no doubt, it's the only way they'd view the arrangement. I thought I was doing the right thing by backing away from her, freeing her to be with someone who suited her better than me. Like the dude who's a friend of her brothers."

"You chose now to have a conscience? You're married to the damn woman. She'd already agreed to everything. Why in the hell would you—Wait, do you feel the same about her?"

Dominic raked his fingers through his hair. "Well, it's too late now."

Trenton exhaled sharply. "Yes, you screwed yourself. Royally. And now you need to fix it. I expect to see you at Mom's this weekend to do just that."

"Oh, so now I'm invited again?"

"Don't push it. Dom, if you love her, she needs to know that." There was less bite and more brotherly counsel in his tone. "Tabitha will likely be there. You can first apologize for making such a stupid mistake, then tell her how you feel about her. If you're lucky she'll give you a chance to make things right."

"Yeah."

But he wasn't confident luck was on his side.

Chapter Twenty

"THERE WILL BE other opportunities. Don't get discouraged."

Evie's comment pulled Tabitha's attention away from her passenger window. They'd left the adoption agency and were now driving the hour-and-a-half stretch from D.C. to St. Michaels, Maryland.

"It's what Ms. Winslow said, but I know adopting a newborn is rare." Tabitha's heart ached almost as much as when she'd lost her own baby. "Just because the couple seemed good on paper doesn't mean they're a good fit. The mother could've at least waited until the interview process was complete before she selected."

"Yes, but him a pediatrician and her a primary school teacher—that's hard to compete with. They already had a 529 plan established years ago in the hopes of adopting." Evie glanced over, her smile soft and encouraging. "Look at it this way: maybe this will give you time to plan as that couple had. You said yourself deciding to adopt was a bit spontaneous. Now you know how to approach it next time."

"That may be, but it doesn't mean I wanted it any less than that couple with their perfect marriage, perfect careers, and perfect 529 college plan." Evie looked at her, and

Tabitha's shoulders slumped. "Sorry. I'm sure they're decent people. It's just upsetting."

"I know, sweetie." Evie reached over and gave Tabitha's shoulder an affectionate stroke.

They rode in comfortable silence for a good distance. Evie cruised the Bay Bridge, crossing the four miles of choppy Chesapeake coastal water. Familiar with the area, having spent summers with her aunt on the bay, she took them along the Scenic Byway with acres upon acres of beautiful farmland, ripened wine vineyards, and majestic East Coast ocean views.

As they drove down Main Street, Tabitha checked out the many picturesque storefront boutiques, galleries, and specialty shops. About a mile out, they routed back along the bay, then turned off the main road and onto a long, private driveway flanked by mature trees. Beyond the thick, leafy branches and immaculate landscaping stood a pristine white two-story waterfront estate.

"Wow! Nice spread the Balaskas have here," Evie remarked.

"There's Kenni." Tabitha pointed in the direction of the three-car garage. "Oh no, she's pacing. That can't be good."

"Nope." Evie shook her head at the sight of their friend talking on her cell phone while trekking back and forth. "Not good at all."

Tabitha instinctively scanned for Dominic's Audi and found relief when it wasn't parked among the line of luxury vehicles.

They exited the car, and Kennedi jogged the short distance to them, pulling them into a hug.

"What's wrong?" Tabitha asked.

"What isn't wrong is more the question." Kennedi scrubbed fingers at her forehead. "Mrs. Shaw is upset because she called Dominic to discuss an issue with their yacht business, Balaska Imperial. They argued. Now he won't be coming out this weekend. Trenton is pissed with Dominic, says his brother doesn't want to deal with their mother's lecturing but needs to suck it up. Mrs. Shaw's taking her frustration with Dom out on their sister, Alizka, according to Alizka. She's even annoyed that Trenton's friend, Vincent, phoned to say he can't make it. It's wild in there. I came out to get some air. Then Brighton Gardens called. I just hung up with the nurse administrator. She said my father's upset because I haven't been by today. He's insisting the staff is keeping me from him. I told him before I left that I'd be away this weekend, but he doesn't remember." Her eyes watered. "I shouldn't have left. He needs me. I've never missed a day visiting him."

"Kenni, it's one weekend," Tabitha said softly and took hold of her hand, offering a supportive squeeze. With Mr. Chase suffering from dementia brought about by a brain tumor, he had good days and bad days. "You've said many times the assisted living facility is top-notch. Your father is in good hands. Try not to worry."

"Can you Skype him?" Evie asked. "Maybe if he sees your face, it would help soothe his concern."

"Oh!" Kennedi perked up. "That's a good idea. I didn't think of that." She whipped out her cell phone from her back pocket and tapped away.

While Kennedi handled matters with her father, Tabitha

used the time to take in the surroundings. With the Chesapeake Bay as the estate's backdrop, she could hear the sound of waves gently lapping at the shore. Colorful flowerbeds in full bloom showcased the front garden. A white stone water feature centered the circled driveway. She imagined Dominic as a boy playing in the water and sunning on the sand. If only she could shake the hurt and be left with the anger.

The call ended. Tabitha turned to Kennedi, who let out a weighted sigh, appearing more at ease.

"I think it worked. He seems fine now that we've chatted."

"Tabitha. Evie. Good to see you." Trenton stepped out of the house. He gave Kennedi a light kiss on the lips before assisting with the two pieces of small luggage. "How was the drive?"

"Not bad," Evie answered as they followed him into a beautifully appointed entryway of off-white marble floors, high ceilings, and fine finishes. They continued forward in the direction of mingled raised voices and entered a large living space. Conversations stopped.

"Everyone, this is Tabitha and Evie. Kennedi's friends." Trenton turned his head to them beside him. He gestured to the woman with long, dark, wavy hair, seated with an erect spine on the edge of one of the twin high-back, powder-blue suede chairs, a cell phone to her ear. "That's my mother. Over there is my sister, Alizka. That's my aunt Gretchen and her daughter, Penny. Aunt Gretch, she's what, a month old now?"

"Trent, she's nearly three months." Gretchen smirked and shook her head.

He shrugged on a chuckle. "They all look the same until they can move about on their own." He looked around. "Where's Grandma?"

"Who knows." Mrs. Shaw sat her phone on the round side table, stood, and straightened her already perfect white chiffon blouse with the coordinated skirt and matching flats. "It's a pleasure to meet you both. Kennedi mentioned you ladies would assist with the wedding plans. I understand you have a business to run, so I've taken the liberty of hiring an event planner. Actually, I just hung up with her."

Tabitha and Evie looked at Kennedi, whose eyes went wide.

"Mrs. Shaw, you didn't have to do that. My friends and I can—"

"It's no trouble."

"Yes, but I—" The doorbell chime interrupted Kennedi's attempt to reason with her intended mother in-law.

"That should be the seamstress here to start the alterations. I'll get the door. Trent dear, show Tabitha and Evie to their rooms. Since your brother has decided not to participate in the family festivities this weekend—" her pink lips narrowed "it's already made up—one of you can take Dominic's room." She linked her arm with Kennedi's and trotted off.

Tabitha, with Evie behind her, followed Trenton upstairs. He directed Evie to the first door on the right of the wide hallway, then led Tabitha to the next room and set her bag on the bench at the foot of the bed.

"This is Dom's old room."

Tabitha strode around the spacious bedroom. She walked

over and opened a set of French doors that led to a private balcony while feeling both relieved and wounded by the possibility of Dominic's intended absence this weekend. "Trent, your brother likely won't be here this weekend because I'm here."

"He was planning to come, but he and our mother got into it *again* over the business."

She turned from admiring the breathtaking view of the bay. Trent was relaxing with a shoulder against a tall armoire, arms folded across the chest of his pressed button-down.

"He's avoiding the lecture about running Balaska Imperial. Our mother can be—" he smiled "—a bit pushy."

"About that. Kennedi doesn't want to wear your grand-mother's wedding dress."

Trenton's head cocked. "But she's getting measured for the alterations as we speak." His brow rose, and he straightened, clarity quickly registering in his gaze. "My mother's getting it altered. Why didn't Kennedi tell me…or even say to her she didn't want to wear the dress?"

"Trent, it's her future mother in-law. She doesn't want to offend her right out of the gate. She also didn't want to upset you."

"Upset me? I don't care what she wears. She could roll down the aisle covered in Bubble Wrap and I'd still marry her."

Tabitha chuckled. "That might be interesting to see."

"Kennedi is the love of my life, my soul mate." His tone grew serious. "Her happiness is priority one for me. I'll have a talk with my mom."

There had been a time when Tabitha pointedly didn't care for him. But he'd since shown himself to be kind, thoughtful, and a caring man who clearly adored her best friend. "Might I suggest you discuss it with Kennedi to be certain on how to go about it?"

"Ah, good point. As for Dom, he told me what happened at your brother's party."

"Well, you know more than me. He cut things off after that evening. I guess you're aware he wants an annulment. I suppose he has someone else in mind to take my place."

"I can assure you that's not the case. He cares about you, Tabitha. I think more than even he realized. He doesn't want to get in the way of you having the freedom to see whoever you choose, like that guy you seemed interested in at your brother's party."

There was a slight accusatory tone as he eyed her closely. "Craig's a friend of my brothers. They'd like to see us get together. But I decide who I want to be with. I'm not interested in him. I thought your brother and I—" She broke off to contain the raw emotions threatening to crush her control. "It doesn't matter. As soon as he returns from Vegas, I'm getting the annulment."

"Might I suggest you give him another chance?" Trenton exhaled. "My brother can sometimes be impulsive."

Tabitha withheld her firm *no*—she didn't need the headache, the heartache—but he delivered a nod. Message received. "I'm going to freshen up. Tell Kennedi I'll be down in a bit."

"Will do."

TABITHA LEFT THE bedroom and went to look for Evie, but her assigned room was empty. She headed downstairs.

The area where everyone had been earlier was now vacant. Three sets of French doors were embedded in the thick wall of glass that offered a magnificent view of the bay. She explored the many rooms. Charming hues of blue, soft yellow, and off-white carried throughout the décor. Ash-gray hardwood floors blended the look. Everywhere she turned, beautiful landscape and seascape photography hung on just about every wall. *Dominic.* Like his bedroom, the entire house showcased his talent.

She continued to stroll the labyrinthine spaces and found herself in a small solarium off the kitchen. The area was warm from the late-day sun rays breaking through the glass. An elderly woman sat erect upon a yoga mat with eyes closed in a lotus position. Relaxing acoustic sounds played from the in-wall surround sound.

"Are you going to stand there or join me?" The woman never opened her eyes.

"Sorry, I didn't mean to disturb you. I was looking for my friend, Kennedi. I'm Tabitha."

"Kennedi, yes. A lovely girl. My grandson did well with her." Her eyes opened, and striking blue irises latched on to Tabitha at the door. "I'm Katerina Balaska. And you are my Dommy's wife, yes?"

Tabitha's eyes fluttered. "I'm sorry, what?"

"I was leaving my room and overheard you speaking with Trent in Dominic's old room. You said you will get an annulment after he returns from Vegas." She surprisingly uncurled her limber body with ease and came to her bare feet. "That would mean you're married to my grandson. He must satisfy the trust clause before he can gain access to his inheritance. And I take it you are the catalyst to make that happen." Her wayward salt-and-pepper curls sprang out of her unruly bun at her crown when she bent to slip on her ribbed footies.

"I was, but—"

"My daughter stood in that very role herself. She hadn't expected she'd fall in love with him." She padded forward. "Such a tragic end Dominic's father suffered." A gentle hand came to rest on Tabitha's shoulder. "As his brother advised, perhaps give him another chance. Dommy can be impulsive." She winked. "My daughter and your friends are in the pool house. I, however, am going to take a long soak." She sauntered out. "See you at dinner."

Wow. Tabitha stood there for a long moment, digesting the woman's words. Dominic's mother had married his father simply so she could satisfy her trust fund. But apparently Mrs. Shaw had fallen for the man.

She made her way to the pool house. Kennedi and Evie sat with Mrs. Shaw at a table piled with wedding books and magazines. Alizka and the others were gone.

"Hey." Kennedi looked up and smiled.

"Tab, have a seat." Evie beckoned to the empty chair across from her.

"Yes, honey, come join us." Mrs. Shaw also waved a hand at the vacant chair. "We're looking at wedding gowns. I postponed the seamstress. We've decided…that is, *Kennedi* would like to purchase a gown instead of altering my mother's dress." She smiled a bit stiffly. Apparently, Trenton and Kennedi had already had *that* talk.

Tabitha took a seat at the table and began flipping through one of the books. "Did everyone else leave?" she asked.

"Trent's in the study catching up on work," Kennedi said. "Alizka, er, Lizzie went to her place."

"Yes, she and her husband, Reid, will return for dinner," Mrs. Shaw said.

They spent the good bit of two hours combing through images of wedding gowns. Then everyone retreated to their bedrooms to prepare for dinner.

The sky had turned a dusky mauve. Tabitha wanted to get a quick run in before dark. It always helped to settle her scattered thoughts. She changed into her athletic apparel. With her workout playlist geared up and pounding through her earbuds, she ran a good length of the beach, kicking sand up with her heels. Her hair and skin slick with perspiration, sweat rolled down her temples and along her spine.

By the time she made it back, the house was bustling with laughter and loud chatter. She eased the entry door closed and skirted upstairs, doing her best to get to her room without being seen.

"There you are."

Tabitha hitched a breath, startled for only a moment. She turned to Evie coming toward her.

"Hey. I've been looking all over for you."

"I went for a run, needed to clear my head."

Evie pushed her glasses up the bridge of her nose, head

angled, studying. "You're okay?"

"Yeah. Looking at wedding gowns and all of the planning just reminded me of when we did that very same thing for me. Don't get me wrong—I'm happy for Kennedi. But thinking about the past, losing out on the adoption, and Dominic breaking up with me... Trust me, that's what it feels like." She took a quiet breath, willing herself for what felt like the hundredth time not to cry. "I got in my feelings a bit, that's all. But all's good now," she hedged.

Evie's soft, warm hand clasped hers.

"Tab, it's me. You don't have to be a warrior. We can stay up here and talk if you want."

Tabitha wasn't about to ruin Kennedi's weekend with drama. "I'm fine." Her friend's concerned gaze didn't falter. "Really." She forced a small smile. "I'm going to take a quick shower and be right down. Tell Kennedi I'll see her in a bit."

"All right."

She entered the room, jumped into the shower, and washed her hair and body at lightning speed. Setting the blow-dryer on high and diffusing her heavy tresses helped tamp down some of the frizz. She dabbed on a bit of lip gloss, then dressed in her periwinkle-blue, sleeveless sheath dress. The cut-out shoulders gave her silhouette an elegant appeal. Her nude ankle-strapped heeled sandals completed the summer evening look.

She made her way downstairs and followed the savory smells into the great room and over into the kitchen. Her foot stumbled. She tried but couldn't swallow, could hardly even breathe. His broad back was to her, but she knew it was him, dressed as he was from shoulders to feet in all black.

Even his well-polished wing tips gave her warm chills.

Among the family chatting and laughing as they crowded the center island counter were Kennedi and Trenton in a conversation with another individual Tabitha hadn't met. Evie chatted with Alizka and a young man, presumably her husband, Reid, along with Aunt Gretchen. There were several other new faces present.

"Tabitha, dear, you're just in time."

She turned her head to Mrs. Shaw entering from the butler's pass-through.

Dominic's head whipped around. Surprise registered in his stare, and she'd have sworn his breathing stalled. She blinked first, then he followed. His lips pursed.

"Dinner's ready, everyone," Mrs. Shaw called and directed everyone into the dining room.

Tabitha filed in alongside Evie. "Why didn't you tell me he was here?" she whispered as they took a seat side by side at one of the twenty-two elegantly dressed place settings with filled champagne glasses.

"He arrived not five minutes before you came down," Evie whispered back.

Tabitha regarded the pretty brunette who Mrs. Shaw had linked arms with and who was chatting at her ear.

"Larissa, you sit here," Mrs. Shaw said, her smile beaming about as bright as the sun as she directed the young woman next to Dominic, who sat directly across from Tabitha. "You two used to be inseparable."

Can she be more obvious? Tabitha now understood why she wanted her son to show tonight. It had little to do with Balaska Imperial and everything to do with Larissa. She'd intended to play matchmaker.

"Good evening, Tabitha."

Tabitha slid her gaze in the direction of those quietly spoken words. His eyes dipped briefly to the bracelet on her wrist then back at her. All she could do was stare at him as her bruised heart welled. Evie's light kick under the table broke her trance. She took a sip of her water while, across the table, the two fell into an easy chat as if they were longtime friends. Partners. Lovers. *Ugh.*

She shifted her focus away from the pair and met Kennedi's sympathetic look. Two seats down from Trenton, a young man stared back at her. He was the only blond in the room. He smiled and delivered a nod. She did the same.

Mrs. Shaw stood at the head of the table with her champagne glass raised, drawing everyone's attention. "Let us give a toast to Trenton and his lovely fiancée, Kennedi."

Tabitha took a deep swallow and concentrated on the dinner presentation laid out before her. Platters and bowls were passed around. The menu consisted of marinated lamb with garlic and rosemary, roasted red and yellow cubed potatoes, cucumber and cherry tomatoes topped with black olives and feta cheese and tossed with olive oil, and spinach with pine nut phyllo tart. There were also crispy, seasoned flatbread squares and a host of other palatable options. It all looked and smelled delicious, yet suddenly she didn't have a taste for any of it.

"You don't like the food, dear?"

Tabitha looked up from the cherry tomato she'd been pushing around on her plate to Katerina Balaska beside her. "I'm not very hungry. An upset stomach," she hedged, though it wasn't a complete lie. Watching Dominic and Larissa had started twisting her belly into knots.

"Ah." Katerina nodded. "Greek cooking can be rich. Eating light is always best after a run."

Tabitha drew back. Did the woman have cameras hidden somewhere or something? She forced herself to consume a small portion.

Following dessert, everyone helped to clear the table, then retreated to the family room.

A short time later, Tabitha looked up when Dominic came to his feet. He hadn't spoken to her since his attempt at dinner.

"I'm going to call it a night," he said.

"But it's only a little after nine." His mother's eyes darted from him to Larissa. "Surely you can stay up a bit longer. Larissa took the time from visiting her family to come tonight. You wouldn't want to be rude."

Dominic smiled at the young woman. "Glad we could catch up." He turned back to his mother. "I got in this evening from Vegas and drove straight here. I'm exhausted."

"Well, you'll have to sleep on the sofa in the library." Her tone conveyed an edge of irritation. "You said you weren't coming this weekend, so I gave Tabitha your room. All the others are occupied as well."

"Then I guess I'll be sleeping—"

"In your room with your wife, I would assume."

Tabitha's head jerked to Katerina Balaska, who'd spoken from her chair over by the window. The elder woman returned her an innocent shrug.

"What wife?" Mrs. Shaw snapped to her feet. "Mom,

what are you talking about?" Her head rotated from Tabitha to Evie, then back to Tabitha, no doubt because Dominic was staring directly at her. "You two are married?"

"Yes," Dominic said without pause, without blinking, without breaking his stare.

"Trenton, you knew about this?"

He answered with a nod, and his mother gaped. That stare—or more to the point, her glare—landed back on Tabitha.

"Is this some kind of a joke? You two hardly said a word to one another. How can you be married?"

"I—" Tabitha started.

"Georgina, stop with the dramatics." Katerina came to her feet. "They're having a disagreement, as young couples tend to do."

"Mom, I'm not being dramatic. Is it wrong of me to want to know why my sons would withhold something as important as this from me? Apparently, they confided in you." Her features furrowed tight. "Dominic Savino, I deserve an explanation." She all but stamped her foot.

Dominic started toward the stairs. "I'm too tired to get into this right now."

"Good evening. We haven't been properly introduced. I'm Eaton."

Tabitha turned her head to the handsome, blond man who'd been staring at her all through dinner. She shook his outstretched hand, and he brought the back of hers to his lips.

Dominic stopped short. "Eaton, what the hell do you think you're doing?" He stalked over and took Tabitha's hand in a firm hold, then continued his wide, determined stride, scooping a black duffel bag from the floor.

She allowed him to trail her along only because it got her out of Mrs. Shaw's line of fire.

When they made it to the bedroom, she slammed the door. "You're not sleeping in here. I suggest you go find out where Larissa is staying and bunk with her since you two are so chummy, laughing it up all damn evening."

"Should I have given her my number when I thought you weren't looking instead like you did with Craig?"

She frowned. "What? I didn't give Craig my number."

"The hell you didn't. I saw you." He moved to the bench at the foot of the bed and took off his shoes.

Tabitha tried to recall what he was referring to as she slipped out of her heels. It hit her. "He sent me a spicy white chili recipe he found on Pinterest that they make at the firehouse."

"Which meant you had to give him your number for him to do so." His lips thinned while he unbuttoned and peeled off his button-down, followed by his undershirt. "The dude's creative. I'll give him that."

She couldn't help admiring his sculpted upper body. "Well, I did it for the recipe. I can't control what he does."

"Look, I don't care about any of that anymore. I don't even know why I brought it up. What's important is I came here so we could talk. Think we could do that?" He stripped down to his black boxer briefs.

She stiffened; a wave of fierce, hot anger sharpened. "Where are the papers for me to sign so I can put an end to this marriage? That's about all we need to talk about. And I said you're not sleeping in here."

"Oh, I most certainly am. I'll sleep on the floor. But I'm not leaving until we talk everything out."

"Give me the damn papers."

He grabbed the duffel bag stationed just inside the door and marched to the bathroom. "After I take a hot shower."

Tabitha took the minutes to undress and change into a tank top and boy-shorts-style panties. She grabbed her comb, climbed in bed, and began working her frustration out on the tangles. She paused, breath catching, when he stepped out of the bathroom wearing only hunter-green boxer briefs. He froze for a moment, his eyes meeting hers from across the room. Damp hair stood at unruly angles. Wide shoulders, swollen pecs, and a ribbed abdomen—a terrain she'd charted so familiarly.

Her gaze drank him in before she brought her stare back to his. "Where are the divorce papers?"

"I don't have them." He came forward and circled to the vacant side of the bed, taking a pillow. "You have a right to be upset with me. All I can say is, I'm sorry. I hope you allow me the chance to show you just how much. Whatever it takes, I will do it."

Weariness was evident in his heavy lids as he dragged the blanket from the foot of the bed, spread it on the cool, hardwood floor, and stretched out his bulky frame.

She could barely control the tightness in her throat as she finished her braid and secured her hair within the satin wrap, then turned off the light. But his constant shuffling about prevented her from falling asleep, that along with her jumble of emotions. She sighed and flipped the light back on. "Get in bed." He sat up, and she flung a gesture at the empty space beside her. "You keep to your side, and I'll keep to mine."

He slid in next to her and brought the cover up to his shoulder, turning his back to her. "I love you, Tabitha," he said quietly, sleepily.

Air seized in her lungs. She took an unsteady breath and let go a slow release, followed by another as she stared at his back. Anger and frustration—she wanted to hold on to those hot emotions that gave her strength. She flicked off the light, bringing the room to darkness, and stared up at the ceiling, denying herself his sweet words. But her eyes welled full and spilled over as a longing to feel his closeness overtook her. She cleared her throat to hide her crying and dried her cheeks against the pillow. "You said you'd never hurt me."

He rolled over, and a warm thigh brushed hers. An arm slipped slowly, tentatively across her body as he spooned himself snug against her. "I'm sorry. I thought I was doing what was best for you. It was a mistake. I realized that. In Vegas, I shouldn't have judged you. I didn't have the right. Knowing what you've suffered through, that you would still want to offer your heart to a child is remarkable. And ending things between us in the cold way I did after all we've shared was wrong. Again, I'm sorry. How do I make this better?"

The feathery soft kiss he brushed on her cheek provoked feelings she feared should remain guarded. But she'd missed his kiss, his touch, his everything. She turned into his comforting warmth and wrapped her arms around his neck, coaxing him on top of her as their tongues dipped and danced. They tugged at each other's clothing, quickly ridding them of any barriers, and easily joined skin to skin.

Good. He felt so good. Tabitha rocked her hips, taking him deeper and deeper still, losing herself in dizzying sensations. Together their dams broke, sending them into a shuddering heap.

He moved off her and tucked her in close. After a long moment, his choppy breathing calmed. "I love you."

"I love you, too."

Everything inside Tabitha settled on the ease of a sigh.

WHEN TABITHA WOKE out of a heavy slumber, it was to a strange, repeating clicking. She heard movement, but the sound appeared to be coming from outside. In the darkness, the coolness at her ankles confirmed the other side of the bed was empty.

She slipped on her robe, then peeked around the shade at the door before stepping outside to the balcony. With his back to her, wearing only his underwear, Dominic aimed a camera at the pink moon hovering over the bay, the long lens zooming in and out.

"Hey," she said. "Couldn't sleep?"

"I guess my body is confused by which time zone it's in. I didn't mean to wake you."

The tide rolled and rippled along the shore, scattering the moonlight across the water. "Your home is beautiful." She looked over her shoulder to find the camera aimed on her and ducked. "Goodness, don't! No way am I camera-ready at three in the morning."

"You're beautiful." He caught her wrist when she tried to dash inside. "Come here." He positioned her at the railing, then turned her to face the bay. "Perfect. Just like that. Now look at me again over your shoulder."

Tabitha reluctantly followed his directive. "I hate taking pictures even when I consider myself put together. Wait." She snatched off her scarf and reset her pose. "Make it quick."

He worked to get the right angle, snapping rapid shots, then studied the image on the camera's viewscreen.

She leaned in to get a look. "Wow, the moon looks even prettier there."

"I added a soft backlight to enhance the shadows."

"It's beautiful."

"You're beautiful." He took her hand and they went back to bed, their limbs twining together in a familiar, intimate sprawl.

Sharing her pillow, with his head tucked close to hers, he pressed a soft kiss on the back of her neck. "I don't want an annulment," he said into the darkness.

"Okay, neither do I."

"I mean, not now and not in six months. I want you, Tabitha. I want to be with you, play a part in the adoption, all of it."

Tabitha swiveled her head to stare at him, though she was unable to fully see his face. "I wasn't chosen. The mother decided to go with a couple." She turned, and he enveloped her in his strong arms.

"Love, I'm sorry. I know how much that meant to you. We'll keep applying."

She lifted her head from his chest. "Dominic, there's still time for you to gain the full amount of your trust fund. You could find a woman who—"

His kiss quieted her, a gentle brush of his lips against hers that soothed any desire to question him. His hands skimmed down her body as he eased her onto her back and came over her.

"I want you. Will you marry me…again, Tabitha?" he asked between tender kisses.

She could neither measure nor express her happiness in that moment. "Yes, Dom, I'll marry you…again."

His smile played across her lips before he plunged his tongue within.

Chapter Twenty-One

*B*ACON. TABITHA CAUGHT the whiff of hickory-smoked bacon on her way downstairs. She entered the kitchen. Evie stood at the center island, which was loaded with freshly cooked bacon, sausage, waffles, fluffy pancakes, and a host of other breakfast foods.

"Sleep okay?" Evie asked, her eyes bright, wide, and questioning. "You and Dom?"

"We're good. More than good." Tabitha came alongside her. "He asked me to marry him," she whispered, smiling while snagging a sausage link.

"You're already married."

"Yes, I know. But this time it's for real, legit." She looked at the food. "Someone's been busy. Where's everyone?"

"Having breakfast outside on the patio."

"There you are, sleepyhead."

Tabitha turned to see Mrs. Shaw entering from outside and wearing a surprisingly welcoming smile. "Good morning."

"Hope you're hungry. There's plenty. Help yourself." She started a new carafe of coffee.

Tabitha exchanged a look with Evie, then studied Mrs. Shaw as she bobbed about the kitchen. Her cheery countenance was a stark contrast to the evening before.

Strong, familiar arms circled Tabitha's waist. She tipped her head back and looked up into loving eyes.

"Hey." Dominic brought her chin up and touched a soft kiss to her lips.

"Okay, you two lovebirds." Mrs. Shaw chuckled.

"Mom, you're in a good mood. She always cooks a spread when she's happy," Dominic remarked.

"Of course I'm in a good mood. Both my boys are happily settled with lovely, accomplished young women. And you, in particular, are on your way to getting your trust."

Dominic exchanged a look with Tabitha. Both prepared to deflate her balloon a bit.

Tabitha accepted the cup of coffee Mrs. Shaw handed her. "Thank you."

"My pleasure, dear." She delivered Tabitha an affectionate touch on her cheek. "I was upset, but I soon realized that everything has worked out as it should. Well, you'll have to wait until Tabitha is in her first trimester—"

"Mom, Tabitha and I would like to talk to you about that."

"I grumbled about it when I first saw the clause at age twenty-three. Well, you have time. A year. Not that you'll need it." She winked. "We Balaskas have strong genes. I can't wait to spoil my first grandchild," she said cheerfully on her way out to the terrace with a full carafe, but Dominic caught her wrist.

"How about I take that out for you, Mrs. Shaw?" Evie retrieved the coffee and went outside.

"Now what is it?"

"I'm denouncing the trust."

Mrs. Shaw looked between them, then she laughed. "You and your teasing."

"Mom, I mean it." Dominic held her stare. "I won't satisfy the trust clause as it's written. But it doesn't matter."

"Of course you will. You're married. The rest is easy." She grinned.

"I can't have children, Mrs. Shaw." Tabitha held her breath, and Dominic wrapped an arm around her shoulders as they watched reality register on the woman's face.

"I love Tabitha. One day we'll adopt. Until that time comes, we're going to focus on each other."

A deafening silence reigned as she flashed a look between them. "I see."

Tabitha cringed at the cold, hard glare she received, then without another word, Mrs. Shaw left the kitchen and went upstairs. Tabitha turned in Dominic's arms and buried her face against his chest. "Great. Now she hates me."

"She doesn't hate you. She just needs some time to digest everything."

THAT AFTERNOON AND throughout dinner, Mrs. Shaw made tepid responses and gave Tabitha weak, if not forced, smiles.

When it was time to depart on a beautifully bright Sunday morning, Tabitha put her bag in Dominic's car and hung back while he spoke to his mother a few feet away.

"I think she's taking it pretty well."

Tabitha looked at Evie. "I think it's safe to say I won't win any daughter in-law of the year awards. Dominic and I agreed, instead of him denouncing his trust completely, he'd settle for the small portion and turn it over to his mother to help their family's business. He also plans to oversee Balaska Imperial and Alizka has agreed to run the day-to-day. That should please her a little."

Dominic turned with his mother and looked her way.

"I should get going. I'm going to stop by my aunt's on the way home." Evie hugged her. "We'll catch up later." She got in Tabitha's car and drove off.

Mrs. Shaw approached. "Tabitha, I want you to know despite how I reacted when I learned that my son had gotten married without my knowledge and that he won't be fully exercising his trust fund, though to do so would help to stabilize and strengthen the family business—"

"Mom," Dominic scolded a warning.

"Welcome to the family." She gave a long sigh and took Tabitha's hand. "It does please me to know my son is happy, that you make him happy."

"She makes me more than happy." Dominic moved to Tabitha and wrapped a comforting arm around her shoulders. "She's the love of my life."

"I love your son, Mrs. Shaw."

"Ooh, come here." She pulled Tabitha into a hug. "And call me Mom."

Tabitha accepted the olive branch. "Okay."

Chapter Twenty-Two

"HERE, LET ME do it. You take a seat." Kennedi took the bowl to finish putting together the fixings for the pesto pasta salad.

"Yes, Tab, you sit. We got this." With her head bobbing to the cool tunes of Tame Impala's "Instant Destiny" pumping from the surround, Evie flipped the shrimp skewers on the grill top then stirred the garlicky quinoa simmering over a low burner.

"Evie, careful. That cooktop gets much hotter than the dial indicates. I need to upgrade the appliances." Tabitha had moved into Dominic's place. She sat on the barstool at the kitchen island and looked on as her friends helped to prepare dinner for her and Dominic. "I just want tonight to be perfect."

"It will be." Kennedi grinned across the counter.

The oven timer beeped. "The pie should be done." Tabitha started to rise. "Whoa." Like clockwork, the waves started again. She swallowed repeatedly. It seemed to be the only way to combat the ebb and flow of her stomach.

"You stay put. I got it." Evie grabbed the oven mitts and took out the blueberry cobbler.

Tabitha pressed a damp palm to her warm forehead. "I

don't recall it ever being this bad the first time. It's nearly seven in the evening. Whoever coined the term morning sickness should be slapped." Her nausea tended to come in intermittent bursts throughout the entire day. She even woke up in the middle of the night liked she'd been out all night and was hungover.

"Maybe it's a good sign that this pregnancy is starting out far different than the last time," Evie remarked and smiled.

"I wonder how you managed to keep it from Dom? Six weeks is a long time," Kennedi commented.

"He's been in Dubai for three of those. But it's been difficult these past few weeks since I find myself hovered over a toilet around the clock." She stroked her stomach in both elation and fear that she'd been given another chance. "I was afraid to get his hopes up…*my* hopes up. I'm not out of the woods, but my doctor says everything looks good."

Evie turned off the burners. "What a wonderful birthday gift to share with him. And he'll now be able to get the rest of his trust fund. I wish I could see the look on his face when you tell him."

Apprehension flared. "I'm not sure how it'll go. It's not like we planned it. I didn't think it was even possible, really. Though he didn't have the funds to participate as a partner, he likes that Trent has made him the front man for the Dubai condo project. And you know he'll have his own photography gallery at Shaw-D.C. when it opens. We've gotten into a comfortable routine these past six months. It's been really good with just the two of us."

"Tab, think positive," Kennedi said.

"Regardless, you won't be able to keep it from Dom much longer," Evie added.

"Keep what from me?"

Their heads turned to Dominic entering the kitchen. Tabitha swallowed a lump along with the queasiness as she eased to her feet and cut the music. "Hey, babe, you're early. I wanted to have dinner ready before you got home."

His gaze darted between Kennedi and Evie. "Evening, ladies." Then, his stare met hers again, and filled with concern. "Is there something you'd like to tell me?" He looked around again.

"We probably should go." Kennedi rounded the island.

"Yes." Evie followed.

Each gave Tabitha a hug on their way out. Alone with him, she said, "Have a seat."

"Tabitha, I already know. Well, I think I do." He brought her into his arms. "I've just been waiting for you to say it. You stopped getting up at the crack of dawn for work. You even skip days of going in altogether. You're up throughout the night. You're my wife. Of course I could tell something was off."

"My goodness, why didn't *you* say something?"

"It was damn hard not to. You have no idea how difficult it's been for me to keep to my lane. To the point, I was afraid. Knowing what you said you went through before, I didn't want to pressure you." His soothingly warm palm stroked her stomach, and his smile went wide. "We're going to have a baby." He touched a sweet kiss to her lips.

"I'm not out of the woods yet." She smiled just as wide. "But yes, we are."

"Who could've fathomed we'd be here six months ago?"

Her gaze tethered to his. Her heart was so achingly full, her joy so profound, it soaked down to her very bones. Everything she'd ever wanted was right there, secured within their tight embrace.

"I don't know, but I'm happy we are."

THE END

Want more? Check out Kennedi and Trenton's story in *See Me*!

Join Tule Publishing's newsletter for more great reads and weekly deals!

Acknowledgments

My deepest thank you to my awesome editor, Julie Sturgeon, for helping me shape my story. I appreciate your tremendous eye for storytelling. Tabitha and Dominic are wonderfully captured in a way that makes them and their world come alive. I had the fortunate opportunity to work with you on past projects and was thrilled to team up with you once again. You're terrific!

Julia Ganis, thank you for providing initial rounds of copyedits. It's always a pleasure to work with you.

I can't say enough how much I love my cover. Leena Hyat, thank you for patiently taking the time to make sure it was exactly what I'd envisioned.

Thank you to Jane Porter, Meghan Farrell, Nikki Babri and the entire Tule Publishing team for being an amazing group to work with, for giving me such a warm welcome into the Tule family, and for the countless dedicated hours of hard work to help bring to fruition my Tycoon's Temptation series.

My heartfelt thank you to my family for their constant cheers.

Finally, dear readers, I'm immensely grateful for your continued support. I'm eager to share more amazing stories with you.

If you enjoyed *Catch Me,* you'll love the next book in….

The Tycoon's Temptation series

Book 1: *See Me*

Book 2: *Catch Me*

Book 3: *Coming February 2021!*

Available now at your favorite online retailer!

About the Author

Award winning author, Michele Arris, has always had a fondness for romance and happy endings.

"I love to write stories where my characters are guaranteed their happily ever after."

When Michele isn't seated in front of her computer, shaping bad-ass alpha heroes who meet their match in strong, hardworking heroines, she enjoys reading all types of romance genres, watching period classics, actually looks forward to working out, which is where she spends time coming up with a lot of her story ideas, is a vitamin junkie, and loves spending time with family and friends – simply enjoying life.

Michele lives in the Washington D.C. area. Get to know more about her by visiting her website at michelearris.com. Find her also on Facebook, Twitter, and Instagram.

Thank you for reading

Catch Me

If you enjoyed this book, you can find more from all our great authors at TulePublishing.com, or from your favorite online retailer.